RELIANCE

Powerless Earth - Book One

Paul McMurrough

Copyright © 2020 Paul McMurrough

British Library Cataloguing-in-Publication Data
A catalogue record for this book is available from the British Library
First paperback edition May 2020
ISBN: 9781838066086

..

FOREWORD

Dyslexia Friendly

As someone who has struggled with dyslexia all my life, it was important to me to release a version of this book in a Dyslexia Friendly format. I understand that dyslexia affects people differently and so the changes to presentation and formatting that I have made may not help everyone, but I do hope that you find it easier and more comfortable to read.

Reliance contains some strong language and themes of violence, and therefore may not be suitable for a younger audience.

CHAPTER 1

Simon stepped out onto the landing and let his apartment door swing shut behind him. Inside, his phone, still sitting on his desk from the night before, silently flashed another missed call. He pressed the button for the elevator.

The elevator car was small, fitting four people at a squeeze, and serviced his block of twenty apartments in the city centre development. Three identical buildings made up the private gated complex, with the river running along the back and a tall iron fence on the other three sides.

Simon stepped into the lift and fixed his collar in the mirror on the back wall. His favourite hiking jacket was getting a little tight. He had the frame of an ageing rugby player and the sweet tooth of a ten-year-old. Thus, the start of his latest fitness push, and now, two weeks in, he was still doing his morning walk to the local shop and the odd 'ease myself into it' session in the gym. He'd stopped playing rugby in his mid-twenties and could count on one hand the number of times he'd seen the inside of a gym in the ten years since.

As the lift doors opened, Simon spied his neighbour, Mrs Fleming, shuffling backwards through the outer door, grocery bags in tow. Her bright green overcoat stretched across her not so slender frame. Simon quickened his step and reached behind her to hold the door but was a fraction too late and ended up in an awkward near Heimlich Manoeuvre.

"Steady on big fella," Mrs Fleming said with a cheeky laugh. "At least buy me a drink first."

Mortified, Simon stepped back, the heat surfacing on his cheeks. "Morning, Janet, you're out early today."

Janet was in her late seventies, he guessed. A retired barrister who lived alone. She seemed to relish his discomfort.

"Can I help you with your bags?" he asked, gesturing at her shopping.

"Don't be silly, sure I'm only going to the lift, but thank you. Ever the English gentleman."

The chime of the elevator spurred her into a wobbling run, her well-worn trainers squeaking on the tiled floor.

"See you later, Romeo," she said with a teasing smile.

Janet took up most of the four spaces in the lift, and as the doors began to close, she gave Simon a warm smile, still chuckling at her own joke.

Simon headed out into the Sunday morning sunlight. He paused at the door and dragged his palm down over his face to wipe away the embarrassment. With a quick shake of his head and a smile, he set off.

It was a ten-minute stroll to the grocery shop, and he admitted he was enjoying getting out for a bit of exercise. Before he'd started his regular walks, he'd have been lucky if the Fitbit his sister gave him registered more than a thousand steps a day.

His daily route took him over the bridge at the train station and down past the old indoor market. But first he had to jostle his way past one of the busiest bus stops in the city. On a weekday morning, there'd be a throng of sleepy commuters spilling out onto the road. Slicing through them became an exercise in polite aggression. Even though it was a Sunday morning, there were still about eight or ten people spread out along the bus shelter.

Simon shook his head in self-righteous dismay, noticing every pair of eyes at the bus stop glued to a phone or tablet screen. On another day, he'd be a hypocrite, but Sunday was a self-imposed 'off the grid' day; no phone, no Internet, no TV. So today, as a non-phone user, he could grumble about how future generations would be social delinquents.

Today, though, it wasn't just the younger people eyeballs-deep in their phones. Everyone he saw had their heads bowed, sometimes multiple heads per screen.

He shook his head. *A generation of robots*, he thought.

Simon reached the bus stop just as one of the new hybrid buses pulled away. Again, every passenger had their eyes glued to their phone, except one girl in a red hat who was waving to a friend outside. The friend returned the wave along with a smile and a blown kiss. Memories flooded back. Simon's heart sank, and his forlorn gaze dropped to his shoes. He could feel the beginnings of a tear collecting. Sometimes he'd see or hear or even smell something that burst a bubble of sadness in him.

A blown kiss had been the last thing he'd seen his wife do as she idled at the crossroads after dropping him off. They exchanged goofy faces, as she waited for the green light and he for the green man, so he could cross in front of her. She won. As her light turned green, she blew him a kiss and pulled away.

Her car got less than twenty feet before a screeching, skidding blur of a delivery van struck her side on. It snow-ploughed her car sideways, then buckled it to rest around a lamppost. The sound of hissing steam, and shouts and cries from bystanders, still woke him some nights. Sarah died instantly.

They fell in love quickly and had looked forward to a long and happy marriage. They got two months.

Sometimes he wished he'd been in the car with her. Life without her just seemed pointless.

The delivery driver later admitted being distracted by his phone and they found him guilty of causing death by dangerous driving. He was now four months into his three-year prison sentence.

As he approached the grocery shop, Simon shook himself from his thoughts. He was a frequent customer of the small grocery store, particularly over the past two weeks. A little bigger than the average corner shop, *Owens' Groceries* had served the local community for over fifty years. Opened by husband and wife, Seamus and Ethna Owens, they ran the shop together until Ethna passed away a few years before. Seamus was still manning the counter but seemed to be feeling the pressure from the big-name chains with their Metro city centre stores.

As he turned the last corner towards the shop, a teenager and then another burst past him, making him stop in his tracks and stiffen.

The youths had come from the grocery shop, from which Mr Owens was now emerging, crimson faced and yelling, and armed with a nasty-looking cudgel. It was a menacing-looking weapon. About eighteen inches of varnished and polished hardwood. It was something that would do a lot of damage, no matter the age of the wielder.

"Come back here again and I'll break your fuckin' legs, ya wee bastards." The foul language didn't seem to come naturally to him, but Mr Owens had had enough of the repeat shoplifters.

Simon approached, tentatively, "Everything alright, Seamus?"

"Wee shite-hawks have been nicking stuff for weeks," he fumed, gesturing with the antique club. "If I get a hold of them, I'll crack their junky skulls."

"Have you phoned the police?"

"There's no point," Seamus said, already shuffling back into the shop, his left leg lagging slightly as an unwelcome reminder of a stroke a few years before.

Despite his age, though, Simon could tell he'd been a fit, sturdy man in his earlier days and judging by his crooked nose, a boxer too. His bent nose sat on top of a grey-white handlebar moustache, which made Simon smile every time he thought of a retired member of the Village People who'd hung up his assless chaps and opened a corner shop.

The shop, or rather Seamus, had a distinctive, not unpleasant smell that reminded Simon of Pears soap. That translucent-gold oval bar that every older relative seemed to have in their bathroom when he was growing up.

"What do you think of this?" Seamus said, pointing to the TV in the corner above the till. "They can't make up their minds if he's dead or not."

"Who? What happened?" Simon asked, looking up at the TV, his brow furrowed.

"They shot Trump last night," the shop owner replied, as Simon scanned the headlines on the ticker along the bottom of the breaking news report.

"Shit, when'd that happen? I hadn't heard," Simon said, staring wide eyed at the ancient TV and reading the various snippets of news scrolling across the screen.

"Last night, about four o'clock in the morning, our time," Seamus replied.

Simon now regretted not having his phone. Instead, he settled for a summary of the events from an excited Seamus.

"An hour ago, they said he was dead. Now they're saying he's in intensive care. These ones don't know what's going on," he said, flicking his head at the news reporters and clicking through the channels with the massive remote until he found newsreaders he recognised. Every station he passed had its own news flash programme, interrupting normal viewing.

"They're saying it was one of the secret service guys," said a voice from behind them.

Another customer had come in while Simon and Seamus had been fixated on the TV. Simon had seen the guy a few times but only spoke to him once when they sheltered in the doorway one day, waiting for a heavy rain shower to die down. They hadn't introduced themselves, but he'd heard Seamus call him Derek.

He joined them at the counter, towering over them both, and focused on the TV.

Derek's attire was a lot more casual than anytime Simon had seen him before. He was usually clean-shaven and dressed in formal trousers with shoes polished to within an inch of their lives. On this occasion, he wore jeans and a grey sweatshirt, and his seemingly weary-worn face betrayed his usual vibrant appearance with its week's growth and eyes cupped by dark shadows.

"The Internet's alive with other theories too," Derek added. "I think he's dead and they're just trying to work out what to do next and how to release the news."

"Yeah, I wouldn't be surprised," Seamus said, settling on a channel and putting the remote under the counter.

The three men stood in silence.

"I'm just gonna grab a few things," said Simon, lifting a newspaper which reported nothing on the shooting, the early print run having gone out before the news had broken.

He paid for his newspaper and a 'crisis' blueberry muffin and headed out, leaving

Derek and Seamus to continue their musing over the unfolding events.

On his way home, Simon was more understanding of the people glued to their phones, but one lap gazing driver still filled him with anger.

Simon threw his coat on the back of the chair and grabbed the TV remote. Normal programming had resumed, but a Breaking News graphic still covered the bottom third of the screen, at least on the first station that came up, which now showed a Sunday morning cookery programme. The graphic cycled through the main headlines.

US President shot at golf club banquet - condition unknown. Then,

White House says reports of President's death inaccurate.

The scrolling headlines listed other key news on a continuous loop;

ISIS claim responsibility for assassination of American President, Trump dead or alive?, Widespread power outages expected overnight, Wall Street trading to be suspended Monday.

Simon switched to Sky News. Here, the lead presenter hosted a panel of political and security experts, each giving their take on the situation based on the little information available.

With regular satellite links to correspondents in Washington and Seattle, where the shooting took place, new and often conflicting information was coming through constantly.

He increased the volume and sat on the arm of the chair, eager to see what he'd been missing.

'... the hospital has refused to comment on the rumour that the President is dead, only confirming that he has been admitted. They would give no further update on his condition. As we know, Kay, a White House staffer tweeted news of the President's death, but they deleted the tweet a short time later. The official line is that the tweet was a very unfortunate administrative error. Could this be the final strange twist of a bizarre presidency? This is Joy Little, reporting live from the Larsson Memorial Hospital in Seattle.'

The presenter introduced a reporter at the White House.

'Good morning Kay, there is still chaos here. The White House press secretary is refusing to engage with anyone from the press corps. It is absolute pandemonium. Since the initial tweet stating that the President was dead and the retraction of that statement ten minutes later, there has been no official statement. In all my years in Washington, I have never seen such panic and confusion.'

The reporter repeated the timeline of events and the cycle of summary and debate, started again in the studio.

Simon moved to his desk, which sat in a small alcove off the living room beside a large window overlooking the murky brown river. He hit the power button, and the familiar hum of the over-sized PC filled the room as his three enormous screens flickered to life.

Each screen displayed various financial analysis programmes and portals, each configured to launch on start up. With a couple of clicks, they were minimised and replaced with a browser window.

Interested to see what the Internet was saying and to satisfy a sense of morbid curiosity, he searched for footage of the shooting. In this digital age, there was a guarantee that such a public event would be caught from multiple angles.

The mainstream news channels hadn't been showing the official footage of the event, but there was bound to be a copy or other sources spreading across the ether.

Simon always wrestled with himself over watching videos of things like this. Watching violent scenes or brutal deaths in movies was one thing — he knew it was just fiction; special effects and makeup, but watching something showing real people in terrifying situations had an effect. There was an immediate sense of shame or guilt for having reduced someone's life-changing event to a cheap moment of entertainment.

There was always the argument that it was news and in the public interest, but he knew it was really just satisfying an innate voyeuristic curiosity.

"Alexa, put the kettle on," Simon commanded over his shoulder as he brought up a search engine. The unmistakable click of the wireless plug in the kitchen was audible immediately at his word.

A quick search returned thousands of potential videos purporting to be of the shooting. Most were clickbait — sites using the event to attract people to their own unrelated content — but he found one that was genuine. He opened the video, which showed a crowd in front of a stage and podium where the unmistakable visage of President Trump stood addressing the audience.

"Nope," Simon winced at the screen, his conscience winning out over his curiosity. "If I watch it, then I can't unsee it." The video of the real-life shooting disappeared at the click of his mouse.

Closing the video window, he got up to make his coffee and returned with a blueberry muffin and an Americano in his favourite Game of Thrones mug.

He sat at the desk and lifted his phone from its wireless charger. The notifications listed thirteen missed calls, six new messages, and twelve voice mails.

CHAPTER 2

Lisa Keenan sat on the edge of the sofa, knees drawn up, comfortably cocooned in her familiar, worn dressing gown. Her latest nameless internet date had left, and his faint scent was all that remained. A sudden memory of the encounter sent a pleasant shiver through her.

She revelled in her confidence, though she momentarily recalled her most recent work performance appraisal. Shaking her head, she thought, *Pisses me off that some arsehole described me as meek! I'm anything but fucking meek!*

Brushing an errant strand of red hair away from her face, she flicked between the news channels. At this time on a Sunday, she should be at Mass, more out of habit than devotion, but not today.

The sudden buzz of a new text message dragged her from her thoughts of the night before.

"STAC: All on-call personnel must report to their designated offices immediately. Reply with acknowledgement and estimated arrival time."

"Ah bollix."

As a communications officer for the Local Government Executive Office, Lisa's nine-to-five involved the drafting of official press releases and emergency announcements, and managing social media content. Feeling that she was going unnoticed, she'd volunteered for the on-call rota for the Scientific and Technical Advice Cell, the emergency body that's activated to give advice in times of national or local crises. Her one and only call up to date had ended up being a training exercise.

What's an assassination in America got to do with us? She thought. But that was above her pay grade, and so she replied to the text and headed for a shower.

Forty minutes later, she flashed her ID to the security guard at the gate and pulled her bright yellow Volkswagen Beetle into the staff carpark. For once, she'd her choice of spots.

Barry Greer, her manager, had arrived just before her and as she approached, he waited and held the door.

"Good morning Lisa," he said, looking up. Lisa wasn't particularly tall, but she'd at least six or seven inches on Barry, which put him at chest height, something she often caught him taking advantage of.

"Hope you'd nothing planned for today?"

"Not really. You?" she asked, fascinated by how a person's hair could be so greasy.

"Nah, just a Netflix and Chill day," he replied.

She looked away to hide a grin; she was sure he didn't know the real meaning of the phrase, but she wouldn't be the one to explain it.

"So, what's this? Another training exercise?" she asked, as they walked together to their office.

"Don't think so," he said. "I'm usually informed before any drills."

"The Trump shooting then?" she asked, brow furrowed. "How's that affect us?"

"Don't know," Barry replied a little curtly. "I'll make some calls." He didn't like being questioned by subordinates when he didn't have the answers. Barry was fine as a boss for the most part, but he could switch to what his staff referred to as 'arsehole mode' in a flash. This occurred more often when senior management were in earshot, and particularly when Barry was shooting down male members of the team.

"Grab whatever you need and set up in conference room two," he instructed, as he stepped into his small, cubical office next to their open-plan room and closed the door behind him.

Lisa placed her bag on her tidy and somewhat sparse desk, which had everything arranged in a neat and logical order.

Pens and pencils were in a tiered plastic holder with battery-operated pencil sharpener perfectly aligned alongside a stapler and hole punch, most of which she hadn't used since being issued them three years ago. It wasn't the 1990s.

The neatness bordered on OCD, something her colleagues ribbed her about. She didn't have the condition, she just worked better in a tidy environment, so she took the jokes in good humour and usually gave as good as she got.

The only personal item on her desk was a black-framed photo showing her seventeen-year-old self, with her parents and older brother, at their farm in Donegal.

That'd been nearly ten years ago. In fact, her mother was planning a big get-together for her dad's 60th that coming Saturday. His birthday parties were always good fun, with the extended family and their parents' many friends included.

Lisa hated having to move desks. She had her set-up just the way she liked it, with her twin monitors above her ergonomically adjusted desk and her chair set at just the right height.

She was a keen yoga student and knew the importance of good posture, so had pushed for months and finally got Barry to sign off on the assessment and adjustments to her workstation. Something which pissed her desk-neighbour off no end. Pete had been trying to get the assessment for about two years with no joy. He didn't have the cleavage needed to persuade Barry.

She unlocked her drawer and found the key for the laptop lock. She unlocked the steel cable securing the laptop to the desk and placed her wireless keyboard and mouse on top. The mouse immediately tried to escape over the edge.

Carrying them slowly along the corridor, eyes fixed on the runaway mouse, she noticed the rhythmic clack of her heels echoing off the pale grey walls.

Lisa was the first to arrive in the cold, dank conference room. *Conscientious*, her school reports would have called her punctuality, merely professional, she thought.

A forgotten coffee cup sat on a side table at the back of the room and was likely the source of the subtle base layer of staleness in the airless space.

The room was basic. A typical government building conference room that looked like it was last decorated in the 70s, except for the jumble of network cables spilling out from a recess that ran the length of the long table and a star-shaped conference phone with four remote mics spidering out across the desk.

She considered where to plant herself. She obviously wouldn't take the seat at the top of the table, Barry's head would explode, so she sat just off-centre with her back to the window which looked out over the carpark. She always hated sitting opposite the window, especially on a sunny day when those across from her would be faceless silhouettes.

By the time she'd arranged her belongings and finally found a network cable that worked, the rest of the team had shuffled enthusiastically into the room, each going through the same seat selection and cable juggling ritual.

She knew most of them only to nod to; they were from different departments or on different floors in her building.

She knew Christine, however; she worked the same office. They weren't friends, by any stretch, but would exchange small talk occasionally in the kitchen or at the printer. The most negative person she'd ever met, Christine always seemed pissed off about something. She took her seat across the table, next to the chair left free for Barry. Bag down, phone out, and chewing on the remains of another wasp. Her role as Academic Liaison involved working with the universities and colleges in situations that required academic input.

Danny Patterson was the next to take his seat. He drifted behind Lisa in a cloud of sinus burning, cheap deodorant which failed to mask the tang of foul body odour. Both he and the chair groaned as he took his place beside her.

"Good morning Lisa," he said, as he squirmed to find a comfortable position. "So what's going on?" His deep, commanding voice resonated even when he whispered.

"Hi Danny," Lisa said with a welcoming smile. "No idea."

Danny was the liaison for the military and Army Reserve.

By the time the room filled, there were representatives for all the major fields; Police and Emergency Services, Food Safety, Local Industry, Utilities, and Public Health. None of them any clearer on the reason behind the call up. The chat around the room, and in small groups, was about Trump and the bizarre way that was being handled in the States.

Twenty minutes had passed and Barry, whose role was to chair the STAC, was nowhere to be seen. Lisa decided to message him.

Hi Barry, just letting you know everyone is now set up in Conf 2. Any news on the purpose of our Sunday get-together? :-), she immediately regretted the smiley face.

On call to London, be there soon. Came the reply. Power outage expected tomorrow. Solar flare.

That did nothing to ease Lisa's confusion. A power outage was hardly something that warranted activating the STAC. She gestured to Danny beside her and angled her screen towards him. He leaned in, a wave of stale beer washing over her. Squinting at the screen, he read the message and shrugged, obviously similarly unimpressed.

Lisa glanced around the room. The team had a liaison for the MET office on the team, but she wasn't sure who it was.

A quick Google search for "Solar Flare" returned a long list of results. Various pages explained the theory behind them, what causes them and their effect on earth.

There were videos and illustrations showing the sun with long trails of fire shooting out from the surface like erupting volcanoes and pictures of colourful lights dancing across the northern skies.

She checked under *News*. The first link that caught her eye was a report from the BBC, published just thirty minutes earlier. The headline read *CME to cause major blackouts*. She put one of her wireless earphones in and opened the video.

The interview was from the regional station. A familiar reporter introduced her guest as Professor Martin Monroe, a lecturer in Astrophysics from Queen's University. He looked exactly as she'd expect a professor of Astro Physics to look, all tweed coat, thick-rimmed glasses and a seriously receding hairline sitting on top of a tomato-red face. *Where were all the Dwayne Johnsons or Gerard Butlers of the physics world?* She thought.

The professor fidgeted with his cuffs, then his tie, then clasped his hands in a white-knuckled embrace as the reporter listed some of his credentials. Evidentially a bigwig on the physics scene. He was impatient to get started.

"Professor Monroe, thank you for joining us. I believe you have some information on a potential power cut due to a solar flare on the sun?" said the reporter, prompting the professor.

"Hello, thank you, firstly it is not a solar flare, well it is, but it's more the CME associated with the solar flare and it is not a potential, it is a certainty," he said in an urgent tone.

"A CME?" the reporter asked, cutting him off.

"Yes, a Coronal Mass Ejection," he said, continuing. "Look, the terms aren't important. The fact is this has already happened and is on an intercept vector, a direct collision course with earth," he said, struggling with the level of scientific language to use.

"But Solar Flares and these CMEs are not uncommon, right? They cause the Northern Lights at the North Pole, don't they?" asked the reporter, having done the bare minimum of prep before the interview.

"Yes, I mean no, they're not uncommon, but this is like nothing that we have previously observed. It is of orders of magnitude larger than anything that has ever hit earth before," said the professor, getting frustrated at not being able to get his message across without interruption.

"And, correct me if I'm wrong, but it isn't something physical, like a meteor or something, that will crash into the earth? So why should it concern the public?" she asked in a slightly dismissive tone.

"No, look, you're not getting it," he said, leaning forward on the desk shaking his head and glancing around at unseen crew or floor managers, as if to protest at the level of idiocy of the reporter they had asking the questions.

"This is much worse than a meteor hitting the earth. Overnight, the world will return to a pre-industrial state. There'll be anarchy, starvation, and disease. Nobody is listening. You must put this out on all the news channels."

"Okay, Professor, I see that you feel very passionately about this, but I think perhaps you're overreacting a little. And I imagine the news stations are rather busy at the moment with more important news."

"There is nothing more important than this," the professor shouted, slamming his hand on the desk. "Nothing will work after tonight..."

"Now Professor, let's not alarm people. We've all been through power outages in the past. I'm sure the authorities and the utility companies will work hard to minimise any disruption," the reporter continued, trying to calm the situation.

She was likely getting instruction in her ear to wind the interview up, the director in the control room likely giving a dressing down to whoever had booked this nutty professor.

"There is nothing more important, you need to warn people..." shouted the Professor, now bouncing in his seat, veins seconds from exploding.

The camera switched solely to the reporter as she tried to wrap up as gracefully as she could. The Professor could still be heard in the background, complaining that they must listen and take the threat seriously.

Lisa doubted that they'd air this interview on the local TV news, never mind the national news. *Another David Icke moment*, she thought, remembering the disgraced TV sports commentator that her dad had shown her clips of.

The video ended and just as she was about to close the window; she saw that the next suggested video was of the same professor.

This was a self-published blog on YouTube and showed the Professor at a desk in front of a stacked bookcase. He was in, what looked like, his pyjamas. *Way to not look crazy, Prof.* she thought. But she clicked play anyway.

Again, the professor looked nervous and alarmed. The video started with him stating again that a Coronal Mass Ejection event had occurred early Sunday morning and would likely reach Earth late Sunday night. He explained that the CME was over 1000 times larger than the biggest to have ever reached earth before, which was in the 1850s and that it would cause catastrophic damage to all power grids across the entire planet.

Just then, Barry entered the room. He paused to make sure he was noticed, then took his seat at the head of the table. Lisa took her earphone out and paused the video. The rest of the room gradually quietened and waited expectantly for Barry to explain why he'd pulled them away from their Sunday routines.

CHAPTER 3

"Okay everyone, thank you for getting in so quickly," said Barry, addressing the room. "It's been a little hectic this morning trying to get a clear picture of the issue, but I'll bring you up to speed with what I know so far. But first, let's do a quick round of the table to see who we have. Please state your name when I call your role."

From a list, Barry called out each of the roles on the team. By the end, only two people seemed to be missing or late, the Food Safety Liaison and the MET Office liaison.

Barry turned to Christine, who occupied the chair on his left. "Christine, when we're done here, would you mind trying to contact these two and find out where they are?"

Christine hesitated, the thunder building on her face. "Ah. Yeah. Okay," she said, making a note in her book. She looked poised to protest, then thought better of it.

"This morning the government received reports from the European Space Agency warning of a potential space weather event which may cause disruption of the power grid," said Barry, addressing the room.

"This is the official statement from the ESA," he continued, lifting a printed sheet from his folder.

"At 03.00 GMT, the Muon Spaceweather Telescope for Anisotropies in Germany, observed a Solar Flare and Coronal Mass Ejection event on the surface of the Sun. Other facilities within the European Space Weather Programme have confirmed the event. The ESA are working together with NASA, FSA and other agencies to analyse the data received and assess the potential risk to infrastructure.

Initial observations, however, indicate that the event is significant and is on an intercept vector with Earth. Authorities are advised to mobilise the appropriate emergency and advisory committees and standby for further updates."

"So, nothing to do with the shooting then?" asked a voice from down the table.

"Nope, nothing at all," said Barry. "That's all we have at the minute. There's an update call scheduled for 2pm with ESA. We should know more after that."

"Is there any kind of public statement planned yet?" Lisa asked. "Should we be drafting something?"

"No, absolutely not. This information does not leave this room until we know more," said Barry, closing his folder and standing to leave. "I need to get back on a call. I'll let you know when we've some further info."

"What do you want us to do in the meantime, Barry?" asked a long, thin mop of a man, all arms and legs and carrot curly hair.

"As I said, Greg, I will let you know when I have more information," Barry snapped. "In the meantime, just get your stuff ready." Without further comment, he left the room, leaving the group only slightly less confused than when he'd entered.

Greg, now resembling a six-foot matchstick, fumed to his neighbour, "Get your stuff ready? What the hell does that mean?"

Lisa sat back in her chair and looked at the paused image of Professor Monroe. "Christine?" she whispered, leaning forward in the hope of a semi-private exchange. Christine, either unhearing or just being Christine, didn't react. "Christine?" Lisa repeated, raising her voice more than she wanted. Christine looked up with a fake smile and raised eyebrows. "Have you ever heard of a Professor Martin Monroe from Queen's?"

"Ha, that nut," Christine said. "What about him?"

"What do you know about him?" asked Lisa.

"He's a total conspiracy nut," Christine replied with a sneer. "He was on the radio a few years ago claiming that aliens were hiding in a spaceship behind the Hale-Bopp comet. Had a nervous breakdown when it turned out to be crap."

"But he's still in Queen's University?" Lisa asked.

"Yeah, Astrophysics," said Christine, staring intently at her phone, no interest in continuing the conversation.

"I'm just watching a video he put out about this CME," Lisa continued. "Might be worth reaching out to him."

"Don't think so," said Christine with a snort as she rose and left the room without another word.

Lisa slowly lowered herself back to her seat, hoping that no one had been paying attention to the exchange. Danny met her with a sheepish look and a coy smile. "That's you told, I suppose."

She stared vacantly at the screen for a moment, "*I'd love to slap the arrogance out of that bitch*," she thought, then pressed play again on the Professor's video.

The video continued, with Lisa pausing it occasionally to make notes. She felt a little foolish, as she watched Professor Monroe stumble through his prophecy of impending doom, wondering if he was actually a crazed conspiracist, as Christine had said, or an enlightened academic who was just so alarmed that he couldn't control his oration of the consequences to come.

In the video the Professor explained how the CME would cause a complete overload of all electricity grids worldwide and that under normal circumstances power grid operators could take measures to protect their equipment but that, in this case, the magnitude of the electromagnetic charge was so great that no amount of preparation would protect the fragile transformers and relays. He predicted that the event would cause a catastrophe that would see the world plunged into the dark ages, from a total breakdown of all electronic communication, transportation, and manufacturing. He warned that, because of modern society's total reliance on electricity, most people wouldn't even realise how things, that they've taken for granted for so long, would cease to work overnight. His video ended with a plea for people to prepare for the worst and use today to stockpile whatever provisions they could, such as canned food, medications, and water.

Lisa closed the video and read over the notes she'd taken. It read like the manifesto of a man who'd taken a break from reality and if it wasn't for the statement from the ESA and the fact that they'd been called in at short notice, she would've taken it as such. But there was still a niggling *what if* in her mind. She looked around the room. Half of the team were on their phones following the unfolding events in the US, seemingly unconcerned by the reason for the STAC's activation.

Greg, the liaison for the utilities industry, was filling a water bottle at the water cooler in the corner. Lisa closed her laptop and strolled over.

"Hey, how's it going?" Greg said as he saw Lisa waiting for him to finish.

"Yeah, not bad," she said with a smile. "Tell me this Greg, if there was a power cut because of this CME thing, what would the electricity companies do? How would they handle it?"

"Wouldn't worry too much. They've procedures in place for this type of thing," he said, screwing the top back on his bottle. "It might cause a short-term supply issue and possibly an outage for a few areas, but they normally keep a few replacement transformers in reserve as contingency. So, they'd just swap them in and things would be back to normal in a few hours."

"What about gas and water? Do they rely on electricity?" she asked, a little embarrassed at her lack of understanding of how these most basic of necessities worked.

"Yes, the pumping stations need electricity and water treatment needs power too, but they've emergency generators as cover in case of power cuts," he replied, a little dismissively, making her feel like a frightened little girl who needed reassurance.

Lisa pursed her lips and bobbed her head. "Of course," she said and bent to fill a plastic cup with water that she didn't need. Greg smiled and returned to his spot at the table.

She ambled back to her seat and considered asking a similar question of the Emergency Services guy, but decided against it. The answer would likely be the same, she thought. Hospitals and police stations would surely have generators too.

Drumming her fingers on the desk, she looked around the room, not sure what to do next. She opened the laptop again and stared at the frozen image of the pyjama-clad professor. She got up, deciding she needed a break from the now hot and stuffy conference room, and a trip to the bathroom, too.

As she washed her hands and dried them as best she could under the pitifully inadequate hand-blower, Lisa couldn't shift her thoughts from the Professor's warnings. No matter how much Christine insisted that he wasn't a reliable source of information — and to be fair, what she'd seen of him didn't help — she still thought it was worth at least talking to him.

On her way back to the conference room, she paused as she passed her usual open-plan office and looked in at Barry's closed door. She started to move on, then stopped again. *Fuck it,* she thought, and instead strode over to the manager's door. She knocked twice and eased the door open without waiting for a response.

Barry sat at his desk, feet perched on the edge. He looked up. Noticing the headset, she raised an apologetic hand and silently mouthed a sorry as she retreated. Barry removed his feet from the table and rotated the arm of the microphone away from his mouth, gesturing her in.

"I'm on mute," he said, whispering anyway. "Come in."

She approached gingerly, "It's okay, I can come back if it's not a good time."

"They're all talking in circles," he said, a slight shake of his head and hand in unison, inviting her in, "What's up?"

"I was doing a bit of research into CMEs," she said.

"I came across a professor who seems to know a lot about it." She glanced at the chair and thought about taking a seat. "He did an interview with the BBC this morning and has put a video up about it himself, too. He's from the Astrophysics department in Queen's."

Barry was half focusing on the voices in his headset. "Has anyone spoken to him?"

"No. I asked Christine about him. She seems to think he's not very reliable."

Barry narrowed his eyes. "Ask her to call him. Actually, no, would you mind doing it? See what he has to say. Better still, see if he'll come in," Barry said, moving his hand to adjust his headset again.

"What about Christine?"

"Never mind Christine," he said with a sigh. "I'll tell her to send you his number." He straightened and pulled his chair in, marking the end of the conversation. Lisa nodded and left the room. Pausing outside the door, she closed her eyes and took a deep breath in anticipation of a run in with Miss Congeniality.

Returning to the conference room, Lisa rounded the table to take her seat. It was obvious from the gargoyled face of Christine that she'd received the instruction from Barry. Her reddened face didn't look up from her laptop. Lisa steeled herself for a fight, or at least a sarcastic comment.

True to form, Christine sat stone-faced. She'd make Lisa ask for the number personally. "Christine," Lisa started.

"Yes, I'm getting it for you now," she said bluntly, cutting her off.

"Thank you," replied Lisa. *If you'd just do your job, I wouldn't have to*, she felt like saying.

"I'm telling you, though, you're wasting your time. But if you've nothing better to do..." Christine added.

Another few minutes passed before a mobile phone number popped up in a Skype message on Lisa's screen. Without reply, Lisa jotted the number on her notepad and headed off to find a private space to make the call.

Lisa dialled the number. It went straight to voice mail; she hung up. She didn't like being surprised by answering machines. After sitting for a moment to compose herself, she dialled again. This time, she left a message. She introduced herself, explained why she was calling, and asked him to call her back as soon as he could.

CHAPTER 4

Martin Monroe paced back and forth in front of the locked sliding doors of the supermarket and looked again at the time on his phone. Because of Sunday trading laws, the tills wouldn't open until 1pm, but they usually let eager shoppers in fifteen minutes earlier.

Ha, the irony, he thought, noticing his smart phone was almost out of battery. He thought about going back to his car to put it on charge while he waited for the shop to open. Just then, a broad-set security guard approached, jangling keys in hand, and with practiced nonchalance, engaged the automatic doors with a twist and a kick.

Martin pushed past him with his trolley, barely waiting for the doors to open fully. He'd a list of specific things he had to get and no time to waste. He'd given a similar list to his mother and his brother, Jim. Assuming Jim could convince his wife of the impending doom, they'd all be meeting him at their family holiday home by the lake in Fermanagh.

He found the battery stand at the end of the first aisle and cleared the pegs of the three main sizes. He looked at his scribbled list as a teenage shop assistant with sleep-deprived eyes shuffled by.

"Excuse me," said Martin. "Can you tell me where you keep your candles, please?"

"Yes, I'll show you where they are," replied the youth, all pimples and braces. He angled his body for Martin to follow.

"Just normal candles?" asked the youth, as they arrived at the household bay between the firelighters and matches.

"Thank you," Martin said, as he scooped up an armful of packets of standard six-inch white candles and lowered them into his trolley.

The shop assistant watched with a bemused frown. "You having a seance or something?"

Martin glared at the young man, which he took as his cue to return to his duties. He lifted the rest of the candles and most of the large multi packs of matches and moved on to the next item on the list.

By the time he'd run out of space in the trolley, he had ticked off about half of his list. He'd everything from torches and solar chargeable camping lanterns, to tins of corned beef and processed ham, the latter still in their shipping boxes, which had been waiting in a wheeled cage ready for an assistant to stack neatly on the shelves. *It was a mistake getting the small things first,* he thought, as he balanced the boxes on top of his burgeoning trolley.

He arrived at the checkout just as the operator took her seat and the supervisor unlocked the till. Bang on 1pm. The supervisor and till operator exchanged glances when they saw the overloaded trolley. The operator rolled her eyes in a *just my luck* silent protest.

"You're not supposed to take full boxes, you know," she spat, as the case of tinned meat came to a stop in front of her. "I'll have to take one out to scan it."

Martin allowed the operator's words to pass through him like dust through a chain-link fence. More important concerns were occupying his mind.

Retrieving a couple of discarded cardboard boxes from a stack provided behind the row of checkouts, he packed the smaller items and repacked his trolley on the other side of the till.

The till total already read £218. He didn't care. He'd put it on his credit card, despite the fact his coat pockets were now bulging with bank notes after his twenty-minute raid on the ATM outside. He'd withdrawn the daily maximum from each of his debit and credit cards, all of which would be useless after tonight.

"You expecting World War 3 or something?" the operator said jokingly as she gave him the final total.

He was now red faced and sweating from all the box lifting. "Worse," he said, stony faced. "There's going to be a prolonged power cut. I'd advise you to prepare, too."

"Right,"she said, dragging out the word and glancing at her neighbouring operator, who smiled back mockingly.

Martin returned a few minutes later, after packing his first run into his ageing Volvo Estate. By now, word of the doomsdayer had spread throughout the bored assistants who'd made his quest into a form of entertainment. They took turns making excuses to walk by him as he loaded multi packs of water, flour, dry rice and salt. Finally, he attacked the medication aisle, taking ointments, bandages and general medications by the boxful.

He returned to the checkouts and got the same operator as before. She struggled to hide her dismay at having to serve him again. She folded her arms and sat back with an audible sigh as Martin loaded his trawl onto the conveyor belt.

Her anger, and the sniggering of the other checkout operators, wasn't lost on Martin. He'd had years of people whispering and laughing at him, students and faculty alike. He didn't like it. He worked on loading the belt, visibly out of breath now, his shirt pasted to his back beneath his coat.

"What are you laughing at?" he barked at the girl on the next till, who quickly spun away to face her next customer. "Do you laugh at everyone who buys groceries?" he asked, turning his rage on his own till operator, then on the supervisor walking by.

The supervisor approached. "Everything okay?" she asked.

"It's fine," he said. "Some people just need better manners."

She threw a Medusa glare at each of the young checkout girls and walked on.

The last of his goods now on the belt, Martin repacked the awaiting trolley.

"You can't buy all them," the operator said, pointing to the dozens of boxes of Ibuprofen and Paracetamol making their way towards her on the conveyor belt.

"What do you mean?" Martin asked, still fuming.

"You can only buy two packets at a time," she said with a smirk.

"Why?"

"It's the law," she said curtly.

"So, I could buy two packets, then walk out, walk back in and buy another two?" he asked.

She shrugged and sat back, "Suppose."

"That's ridiculous!" he said, raising his voice again and looking around for someone to talk sense to her.

The exchange now had the attention of other staff and customers, some pretending to look at items on nearby shelves, others blatantly gawking and revelling in the spectacle. Martin slowly turned, meeting each ridiculing face as he did.

"What are you all looking at?" he said, not quite a shout but laced with anger and frustration. He scratched at a recurring patch of eczema at the corner of his eye. "You've no idea what's coming. You all need to start preparing."

The supervisor appeared again at the sound of Martin's agitation.

"Excuse me sir, what seems to be the problem?" she asked firmly, but with a softening of compassion.

Martin took a breath, realising he was losing his cool.

"Look, there will be a major power cut later this evening, and it will last a long time. I'm just trying to buy some things to get me through," he said in a more hushed tone.

"And I'd advise you all to do the same," he added a little louder again, turning slightly to direct his advice to those nearby.

"She says I can't buy more than two boxes of tablets," he said to the supervisor.

"Okay sir, I understand. I didn't know about a power cut," the supervisor said, trying to calm the situation. "Unfortunately, that's the law. We can't sell more than two packets of certain medications at a time."

"Right, okay," he said, shaking his head. The supervisor moved to the next empty checkout and tried to make herself look busy.

The operator stacked the surplus medication by the side of her till and silently finished scanning his items.

After paying for his second load and finishing packing the trolley, Martin noticed the security guard sidling closer, aware of the tension.

Great! Martin thought. Enjoy your last day in work.

He hurried out into the car park, aware that the guard had slowly followed him to the door.

The boot of his car was now packed-high with supplies, and cases of bottled water filled the back seats. With two hard shell suitcases strapped to the roof rack, it looked like he was all set for a family camping trip. As he took his phone out to charge it, he noticed two missed calls and a voice mail notification. He hadn't noticed it ringing with the commotion in the shop. Simon, he assumed. But he didn't recognise the number.

Martin listened to the message and immediately perked up, the altercation in the shop suddenly forgotten.

Finally, someone is taking notice, he thought. He dialled the number left by the caller, Lisa.

CHAPTER 5

Derek Henderson drove under the flag adorned archway and along the narrow street of terrace town houses with its newly refreshed red, white, and blue curb stones. He drove on a little way, then turned into his street, which was less colourfully decorated.

He swung the nose of his black Nissan out before carefully reversing into the tight driveway of his modest, semi-detached house.

He sat for a minute listening to the end of the Sunday lunchtime news. A trio of gnomes stared at him from their overgrown jungle that was his small patch of garden. They seemed to disapprove of how long he'd taken at the shop, while his exhausted wife tended to their new son inside. *Okay, I probably took a little longer than I should have*, he thought. Having a few extra minutes of alone time was a guilty luxury. Juggling the milk, bread, newborn-nappies and baby wipes, he pushed the car door shut with his foot and shook the front door key loose from its bunch.

Inside, he placed the shopping on the antique telephone table and quietly closed the heavy reinforced door, habitually locking the three dead bolts. He peered into the living room on his way to the kitchen and smiled at the sight of the tightly wrapped bundle finally asleep in the small Moses basket in the corner.

"Hey," he said in a hushed tone, "you got him down, then?"

The hissing of the iron, and the sweet arid scent of needlessly expensive ironing water, filled the kitchen.

"Yeah, just about five minutes ago," said Jenny from behind the ironing board, as she hung another of his prison guard uniform shirts on a hanger and hooked it around the handle of the utility room door.

"What are you doing? Leave that and go and relax," he said. "I'll do it."

"It's fine," she said. "I needed to do some bed sheets, anyway."

"I'll do them, GO and sit down and I'll make you a cup of tea," he said more forcefully.

Giving in, she sat the iron upright and slumped into a chair at the small kitchen table. She sat in silence, chin resting heavily on her hand.

"I wish you weren't going back to work so soon," she said with a sigh and an exaggerated frown.

Derek filled the kettle and flicked it on.

He moved around behind her and gently rubbed her tense shoulders with his thumbs. "I'm not back to work till Wednesday."

Jenny was resigned to the fact, but still not impressed. "Hummm."

"It'll be fine. He's starting to sleep better now," he said.

"I'm just so tired. I don't know how I'm gonna cope all day on my own," she said, rolling her shoulders into his thumbs.

"It'll be fine, love," said Derek. "He's getting into a nice routine."

He kissed the top of her head and went back into the hall, glancing again with pride at their new arrival.

As he put his foot on the top of the radiator, he slid the right leg of his jeans up and peeled open the wide velcro straps of his ankle holster with a satisfying rasp. He opened the small cupboard door below the drawer in the telephone table, unclipped his Glock 26 from its holster, and removed the magazine. Carefully ejecting the round from the chamber and thumbing it back into the clip, he placed them both side by side into the compact gun safe, which he'd installed himself. He locked the safe, put the leg strap in the drawer, and returned to the kitchen to make the promised cup of tea.

"I hope you didn't put your dirty shoe on that radiator again," said Jenny with a disapproving but resigned frown. She didn't like the idea of having a gun in the house but had ultimately agreed given the high threat to off-duty prison officers. She shuddered at the thought of anything happening and him not having any way to defend himself.

"Of course not," he lied, hoping he hadn't left a telltale footprint on the radiator. "Right, do you want anything with this tea?" he asked.

"No thanks. Just tea's fine."

"Actually, I might have a beer. The match is on soon," he said, only half joking.

"Ah, I don't think so. You've all this ironing to do, remember," she said, nodding at the clothes basket.

"Alright, alright," he said, rolling his eyes. "But I'm not ironing bed sheets. Who irons bed sheets?"

"Husbands who want permission to watch the football do," she replied, eyebrows raised.

CHAPTER 6

Simon clicked into the notifications on his phone. All thirteen missed calls were from Martin, the first from 5.30am. He'd then called repeatedly throughout the morning. The text messages were also all from Martin. Something was wrong!

05.31 — Simon, call me. Very important!

05.48 — Massive CME. Due to hit tonight. Call me.

06.25 — Simon this is huge, will cause global blackout.

07.20 — Contacted BBC, doing interview this morning

11.15 — Idiots are not taking it seriously!

11.20 — Call me, please.

Simon re-read the messages, then listened to the voice mail messages. The frenetic tone of Martin's voice worried him.

It's not like Martin to be so frantic, he thought.

He'd only heard Martin this emotional once before when he talked about the Hale-Bopp incident. Simon hadn't known him at the time, but from what Martin had told him, a reporter had properly stitched him up. The unethical reporter had edited an interview to make it look like Martin, a young Physics Professor, was endorsing a wild conspiracy theory about an alien spaceship hiding in the comet's tail. Some mainstream news channels picked up the story on a quiet news day, and so his faculty photo was plastered across TV screens as the new poster-boy of the theory. The aftermath took a devastating toll on Martin.

The University was reluctant to support a legal battle that they knew had little chance of success. His colleagues, students, and even people he thought were friends ridiculed him. People in the street would snigger behind his back, or worse, shout abuse in his face.

The story destroyed Martin's credibility as a serious scientist. Understandably, the whole situation had a terrible effect on him personally. He fell into a deep depression, withdrawing from everything and everyone, to the point where he'd barely leave the house.

About six months later, when the comet had finally passed Earth, and it was clear that there was nothing in its wake, a local station recycled the story as a lighthearted end to their news programme. It was anything but lighthearted for Martin. The jokes and taunts started afresh, resulting in a total mental breakdown. He took over a year off work, most of that spent in his parent's holiday home in Fermanagh. He barely spoke to a soul the entire time. His trust in people was gone, as were most of his supposed friends. Even to this day, Simon had the impression that he was Martin's only real friend.

A pang of guilt hit him as he thought of how he'd soon be moving back home. Martin had been so supportive and such a good friend, particularly in the past eighteen months. He would miss Martin.

He put his mug on the desk and moved to the window overlooking the river Lagan. He called Martin's number. Engaged.

As he gazed out the window, he thought about what Martin had said in his text.

How could it be a global power cut? He thought.

He didn't know much about Solar Flares and CMEs. As far as he remembered, they only affected a small area, but this was Martin's field, so he had to assume he knew what he was talking about.

He tried the number again.

"Simon, where have you been?" asked Martin in an urgent tone. "I've been trying to get you all morning."

"Sorry mate, didn't have my phone," said Simon.

"Did you get my messages? This is serious Simon; I mean apocalyptic serious."

"I got your messages. What do you mean, apocalyptic serious?" said Simon, careful not to imply that Martin was exaggerating. "Did you not tell me once that CMEs only affected a limited area?"

"Normally yes, but this one is so much bigger than anything that has ever hit earth before. I'd say it's about 1000 times the size of the Carrington Event."

Simon remembered studying The Carrington Event in university. It was the name given to a CME that hit Earth in the 1850s. Obviously, it was before widespread use of electricity, but telegraph systems in North America and Europe were badly affected and some operators were even electrocuted.

Simon turned from the window and lifted his cup again. "So how long do you think the power will be off?"

"Simon, this's so big that I don't see how they'll recover from it. It's going to be chaos."

"What do you mean?" asked Simon, trying to hide the incredulity from his tone.

"Are you at home at the minute?"

"Yes."

"I'm just about to pass your place. A government committee has asked me to assist them, but I can call in for five minutes. Can you meet me in the car park?"

"Yeah, okay. How long will you be?"

"Two minutes. I'm just round the corner."

"Okay, I'll buzz the gate for you."

Simon hit the button on the key fob to open the main gate as Martin swung his car in.

He walked alongside as Martin pulled into a visitor's spot. He noticed the suitcases strapped to the roof and cases of water stacked high on the back seats.

"What's all this stuff?" he asked, as Martin got out of the car. "You going on a trip?"

"Simon. I need you to listen to me. We need to get out of the city," he said, with the same urgency Simon had heard in the voice mails.

"You think it'll really be that bad?"

"Yes, it will."

"Why has there been nothing on the news or alerts or something?"

"I did an interview this morning on the BBC, but the idiots won't listen. All anyone's interested in is the Trump shooting," said Martin, shaking his head. "Anything that the ESA or NASA is putting out is being overshadowed by that," he added.

Simon frowned and nodded understandingly.

"The government must be starting to understand how major this is though. A girl from some emergency committee just called me and asked me to come in to talk to them about it," said Martin. "So I'm sure they'll be putting warnings out about it soon."

"Right," said Simon, still not sharing Martin's sense of doom.

"Look, I have to go and meet this girl. In the meantime, can you get as much supplies as you can?" said Martin. "Tinned food, dried foods and water, and make sure you fill your car with petrol," he added, moving to get back into his car. "As soon as this's made public, there'll be a run on petrol stations and shops. Get everything you can now and wait for me. Then we can go to the lake house. My mum and Jim and his family will meet us there."

Martin started his engine and buzzed the window down.

"Okay, I will," said Simon. "Are you sure you've space?"

"Yes, there's plenty of room."

Martin reversed out of the parking space. Simon strolled alongside and pressed the button again to open the motorised gates.

"Oh, and get as much cash as you can out of the bank machine," said Martin, as he rolled forward, waiting for the gate to open fully.

"How long do you think you'll be?"

"I don't know, but wait here for me and we'll go together," said Martin.

Simon watched as Martin pulled out of the car park and the gates began their slow closing arc. He scratched the back of his neck and looked around, as if expecting to see other people scrambling to load their cars in a panic to get out of Dodge. He did not.

Nothing had ever given him reason to doubt Martin's side of the Hale-Bopp story, but this all just seemed a bit extreme and he'd never seen Martin act so manic.

He walked back to the door of his apartment block and paused, finger hovering over the entry keypad.

Ah fuck, he thought and instead walked around the building to get his car. Some apartments had their parking space in a shared garage on the ground floor of the building. His was one.

He pressed another fob and the garage door started its slow, rattling ascent. *Just in case he's right*, he thought.

CHAPTER 7

Lisa met the Professor at the main door, having received the call from the security guard, and led him into a small meeting room off the main reception.

She took a seat across from him at the plain grey desk. "Thank you for coming in, Professor, especially on a Sunday."

"Please, just Martin is fine," he said.

"Okay Martin, thank you."

"I'm just glad someone is taking this seriously," he said.

"Well, I saw your video and the interview with the BBC from this morning."

"They hadn't a clue what I was telling them. They just wouldn't listen," he said, scratching again at the dry skin beside his eye.

"Yeah, I saw that. I thought they were very rude," said Lisa. "*I'm* listening now."

Martin stared for a moment, then looked round the small bare room.

"You said you were part of a committee," he said, his raised eyebrows turning the statement into a question.

"Yes, sorry, I'm part of the Scientific and Technical Advice Cell. We're called in to coordinate and advise in times of emergency."

"Okay, so the government is accepting the enormity of the situation?" said Martin with a relieved sigh. "But why have they not warned the public yet?"

"Well, yes and no," said Lisa. "We were activated this morning after a warning from the ESA about a Solar Flare."

"And CME," Martin interrupted. "The CME is the important part."

"Yes, and the CME," continued Lisa. "But there wasn't much detail, and they certainly didn't say that it was anywhere near as serious as you've been suggesting in your videos."

"I am not suggesting, Lisa, I am relaying the facts," said Martin, agitation creeping into his voice again, "and the ESA and NASA and any of the agencies monitoring space weather and Solar activity know exactly the devastating magnitude of the CME."

"So why aren't they issuing stronger warnings about it?" asked Lisa.

"I don't know. It could be due to the fact that it's so much bigger than anything that's been recorded before, and that's making them doubt their readings," said Martin, his pitch increasing. "Or maybe they do accept the readings, but know there's nothing they can do to prevent the catastrophic damage that it'll cause."

He must've realised that he was gesticulating a little too much with his hands, so he placed them flat on the table. When he lifted them again to scratch his face, Lisa noticed ten little damp fingerprints on the tabletop. She'd never seen someone so nervous.

She looked away; it was clear how passionately this guy believed what he was saying, but could she put him in front of Barry and the rest of the STAC team? *Not unless he calmed down,* she thought.

"Can I get you some water?" asked Lisa, as she rose from the desk.

Martin bobbed his head. "Yes, please."

When she returned with two plastic cups, she saw that Martin had taken a stack of sheets from his worn brown leather bag and was arranging them on the desk in front of him.

"Okay, so can I suggest that you give me an overview of the facts and then we can go and see my boss, Barry Greer?" she said.

"We'll need to be very concise, logical and unemotional when we talk to Barry," she said. "Which being a Scientist will be very easy for you I'm sure, but we need to keep it simple and clear," she added, trying not to appear condescending.

"I understand," said Martin, as he took a sip of his water.

"Okay, so how and when did you become aware of this?"

"Space Weather has been my main area of research for the past ten years. As part of that research, I have programmes running constantly that take readings from various satellites and monitoring stations. At 4.37am this morning, I received an alert on my phone from one of these programmes," he said, taking a breath and willing himself to slow down. "I don't sleep very well," he offered with a smile.

"When I saw the readings, I obviously thought it was just an error in the programme. But when I checked it, and then checked the scientific forums, I realised that it wasn't my program. Other people were talking about the readings too."

"Okay," said Lisa, scribbling notes as he spoke.

"So to cut a long story short, the readings confirmed that a Solar Flare on the surface of the Sun had occurred and that a massive Coronal Mass Ejection," he paused, "basically a jet of electrically charged plasma, had been emitted and was on a direct course to Earth."

Lisa folded her arms across her chest, then immediately unfolded them again, conscious of her body language.

"So it's the size of the CME that's the problem?" she asked.

"Yes, it's off the charts. We've never seen anything like this before, and couple that with the fact that it's coming directly towards Earth makes it extremely dangerous. Because of the sheer size and speed of this CME, it will envelop the entire planet," said Martin, painting a picture with his hands.

"So, when will it hit?" asked Lisa, frowning.

"It's hard to give an exact time. A CME would normally take anywhere from one to four days, but the estimate is that we'll start to see the effects any time from around 10pm onwards," he said.

"Tonight?" confirming that what she'd heard him say in his videos was correct.

"Yes, tonight," said Martin, the sense of urgency returning to his voice. "We need to warn people. The government should be putting out bulletins on TV and radio. People need to start preparing."

"Okay, I understand. The lack of direction from ESA and NASA isn't helping," said Lisa, turning both palms to Martin.

"Right, before we see my boss, run me through some of the ways this thing's gonna impact us," she added.

For the next thirty minutes, Martin presented a seemingly endless list of things that would stop working and reasons why they might be out of action indefinitely. Most of which Lisa hadn't even considered.

From the most immediate effects, such as the power and lights going off, to day-to-day problems like mobile phones, ATMs and shop tills ceasing to work.

Lisa glanced down through the list she'd made on her notepad. She wouldn't have thought of a lot of it herself, but when the Professor explained it, it made perfect sense, especially if he was right, and the power would be off for an extended period.

Communications were supposedly to be one of the major problems. Most people used mobile phones instead of landlines, or at least cordless phones in instead of handsets plugged directly into the phone socket. Without electricity, both would be useless. And even for those who had a hard-wired phone, most places that they'd be trying to call, like police stations or hospitals, used modern electronic switchboards, which also needed power.

She could feel a tightness in her chest as the magnitude of the situation began to sink in.

This could be really serious, she thought, if it's true.

"Is there a direct risk to life from the CME?" she asked.

"No, there shouldn't be, not for people on the ground anyway," he tailed off, his eyes widening in alarm, as if realising something for the first time.

CHAPTER 8

Simon's local petrol station had been no busier than normal, a couple of cars queued for the drive-through car wash, and one or two people had shopped for the Sunday papers or last-minute items for Sunday lunch. He filled his tank with petrol, enjoying the sweet forbidden aroma as he'd done in his childhood, and withdrew £200 from the standalone ATM, although he nearly didn't bother when the machine warned him that there would be a 95p charge for the service. *Purely out of principle,* he thought.

A few minutes later he pulled into the small lay-by outside Owens'.

"Back again?" said Seamus when he saw Simon come through the door.

It looked like Seamus hadn't moved in the couple of hours since Simon had last seen him. He was still perched on a high stool behind the counter, engrossed in the repeating news reports.

"I've just been told by a friend of mine at Queen's that there'll be a major power outage tonight and it's likely to last for a while," said Simon as he approached the counter. "You see anything about it on the news?"

Seamus' bushy eyebrows and moustache contorted as if to meet each other and he shook his head. "Oh, there was a line about it across the bottom of the screen at one stage, but no one's said anything."

"Apparently it's gonna be really bad," said Simon. "I think I'll grab some things just in case."

Seamus nodded, happy for the extra business. He sat quietly, glancing from the TV to Simon each time he returned to the counter with various items he thought might be useful in a blackout. Seeing the hoard grow on the counter, Seamus got down off his perch and disappeared into the storeroom, reappearing with a large empty cardboard box.

"Do you have a generator for the freezers if the power does go out?" asked Simon, as he paid for the survival supplies, which, of course, included a four pack of blueberry muffins.

"Nah, but as long as it isn't off for more than a few hours, they'll be fine."

"I don't know. I think it's supposed to be off for a long time, according to my friend," said Simon, pursing his lips. "Do you know anyone who could loan you one?"

"Not on a Sunday," said Seamus, raising his eyebrows. "I'll probably be able to sort something out tomorrow if I need to."

"Well, keep an eye out for some news on it," said Simon, nodding at the TV. "I'm sure they'll put something out if it's gonna affect us."

Simon carried the box out to his car, Seamus followed him to the door with the extra two bags that hadn't fitted in the box.

"Thanks Seamus," said Simon, taking the bags.

"That'll keep you going for a while now," said Seamus with a smile.

"Hope so," said Simon. He put the bags in his car, nodded to Seamus, and drove off.

Lisa waited for the professor to finish, but he sat, frozen in thought.

He stood abruptly. "We have to get them to ground all flights," he said, looking to the door. "the atmosphere will protect people on the ground, but planes in the air will be exposed to massive levels of radiation. They'll be like flying microwave ovens. Passengers will be cooked in their seats. You have to get them to close the airports."

"Okay, come with me," said Lisa, rising from her seat.

She led Martin down the hallway to Barry's office, passing others from the STAC group who milled around, still seemingly oblivious to the unfolding threat.

Barry's door opened before she had time to knock.

"Barry, this is Professor Monroe, who I spoke to you about," she said.

"Ah hello professor, thank you for coming in at such short notice," said Barry, looking a little startled at the ambush.

"Barry, you need to hear what the professor has to say," said Lisa, cutting short the pleasantries.

"I was just gonna nip out to grab a sandwich. Why don't you sit down with the professor and make some notes and we can discuss it with the team in about half an hour," he said.

"I already have," said Lisa, holding her notebook up. "This can't wait, you have to hear this."

"You have to get them to ground all flights immediately," said Martin, the panic clear in his voice.

"Excuse me?" asked Barry with a slight shake of his head and a glance at Lisa. "What do you mean?"

Lisa cut across, "Barry, give us ten minutes," she said a little more diplomatically. "It's really important."

Barry sighed, stepped back into his office, and took his seat again, leaving Lisa and Martin to follow.

Martin cleared his throat to speak, but Lisa beat him to it. The potential issue with the flights alarmed her too, but she knew she better try to control the delivery of the information.

"Professor Monroe has been taking me through what he knows about the CME and there's something that we need to raise immediately," she said.

"I hadn't thought about it before now," Martin added.

Barry glanced at Martin, then returned his focus to Lisa, raising his eyebrows.

"There's a chance..." she started.

"A certainty," exclaimed Martin.

"There is a very high chance that, when the CME hits, sometime later this evening, that airplanes in the air at the time will be exposed to higher than normal levels of radiation," she could see Martin shifting in his seat beside her.

"Fatal levels of radiation," said Martin, leaning forward.

"Okay, okay, relax," said Barry, leaning back and slightly rotating in his swivel chair. He raised his hand, forearm still resting on the desk, apparently not as alarmed as Lisa and Martin thought he should be. "This has already been discussed in London. I'm just off a call and the Cobra committee has been briefed on the potential risk to flights," he said. "They're considering the options."

"And what are they saying about the other likely effects of a CME of this magnitude?" asked Lisa, face reddening slightly at her hijacking of her boss.

"Well, they haven't gone into too much detail on the calls I've been on, but they've a full team on it and are assessing the next steps," said Barry.

"Do you mind if we summarise some things that the Professor has been telling me?" said Lisa, clutching her notebook in front of her.

"Yes, that'd be good, but I'd like the full team to hear what the Professor has to say," said Barry, looking at his watch. "I'll get the team to reconvene in the conference room at 6pm. Does that give you time to put a few slides together?"

Lisa could see Martin squirming in his seat and checking his own watch, but before he could say anything she replied, "Yes, we can do that."

"Good, okay, I'll see you then," said Barry as he pushed himself back from the desk and stood.

Back in the meeting room, Lisa could see that Martin's patience was waning. Checking his phone constantly and muttering to himself quietly, he paced back and forth in the small space as Lisa summarised her notes into a PowerPoint presentation, rechecking some facts with him as she did.

His rubber-soled shoes squeaked with every step. To Lisa it was like fingernails on a blackboard, but she said nothing. He was obviously fragile, and if he needed to pace, she would let him.

She finished her slides and read through them once more for a final seal of approval from Martin. It was 5.30pm.

"We've thirty minutes," she said. "We should get something to eat ourselves. It looks like it could be a long night. Sorry, I'm making the assumption that you're willing to stay?"

"Yes, I can stay, but are these people going to start taking this seriously?"

"I hope so," she said. "There's a petrol station just down the street. We could probably get something there."

"Do you have a car?" asked Martin.

"Yes, I'll drive."

"You should fill it up."

She nodded, "Yes, I will, good idea."

Lisa used the short journey to make a couple of calls. Martin sat in silence beside her, scrolling through message forums on his phone and shaking his head.

"Hi Mum," said Lisa, pointing to her bluetooth ear-piece and giving a brief smile to Martin when he turned, thinking she was talking to him.

"Hi love, how's you? Are you still planning to come up on Wednesday? Your dad's fussing over this party. I preferred it when we did them as a surprise. He told me to remind you to call and pick up that wine he ordered. I don't know why he can't just get it here. That's a lot for you to have to carry."

"Mum…"

"Make sure you get someone to help you out to the car with it now. So, when will you be up?"

Jesus, the woman doesn't take a breath, thought Lisa.

"Mum…"

"Have you been talking to Ray?" her mum continued. "He's working till Wednesday morning, so he'll be here in the afternoon, he says. It's a pity yous can't drive up together. You'd save petrol. It's really expensive in the North."

"Yes, I just spoke to him. Mum, I'm not phoning about the party," said Lisa, a little sharper than she meant to. "I've been called in as part of the emergency committee I'm on."

"What? Why, what's wrong? On a Sunday? I hope they give you a day in lieu for that."

Lisa long blinked in exasperation. "Mum, there's gonna be a power cut."

"A power cut? Have you got candles?"

"No, Mum, listen," she glanced at Martin, who appeared to be oblivious to the conversation. "There's going to be a power cut all over, even up there, so you need to prepare for it."

"Sure, we'll be fine. We've got the wind turbine and I've plenty of candles. I'll set them out, though, just in case."

"Okay, that's good, but I'm working with some experts here," she glanced again at Martin. "They say that this might last for a while. It may even run into days or weeks."

"How many days? What about the party?"

"I don't know, but go out and get in whatever you need now before the shops close."

"Okay, love, do you have everything you need? Are you still working? Don't let them keep you in too late now."

"Okay, mum, I'll see you on Wednesday. Have to go, love you."

"Love you too, bye."

Lisa pressed the button on her headset to hang up. Phone conversations with her mum were difficult, and she always felt a little guilty for letting her frustration get the better of her on the calls.

"You should get as much money out of the bank machine as you can," said Martin, as they pulled into the forecourt.

Lisa's brow furrowed briefly, then she nodded in understanding.

"I'll see you in there in a minute," she said, as she got out to use the petrol pump.

She finished at the pump, withdrew her daily maximum from the bank machine and followed Martin into the shop. She picked the least stale looking pre-packed sandwich from the few that remained on the shelf and looked around for Martin.

He was in conversation with the attendant at the counter. When she approached, she caught the tail end of the grilling Martin was giving the young man about whether the station had a generator, or a hand pump, in case of a power outage. The part-time sales assistant obviously didn't know and seemed relieved when Lisa interrupted the conversation.

"You should get as much supplies as you can," said Martin, when he saw Lisa with just a sandwich. "This might be your last chance."

She took Martin's advice, and with her boot now full of various dried and tinned foods, they drove the short distance back to her office.

CHAPTER 9

In the conference room, Martin sat beside Lisa. Danny having graciously given up his seat for the visitor.

Most of the people in the room were unaware of who this visitor was, but Christine knew him. She was standing with a small group of others by the water cooler as Lisa and Martin entered. With the whispers and laughs, and not-so-subtle glances from the group, Lisa was sure Christine was giving them her thoughts on the professor.

When she returned to her seat across the table, she sat with arms folded and looked anywhere but in Martin's or Lisa's direction.

Barry entered and dropped his laptop and folder on the table with a thud — his usual, *I'm here, look at me,* gesture — which Lisa thought he'd probably learned from some management book. He looked around the room before taking his seat.

"Okay everyone," he said. "Thank you for your patience. I want to bring you up to speed on what we know so far."

The room slowly came to order, whispered conversations put on hold. People were eager to hear the latest, and hopeful that the situation was less serious than first thought so they could get home to their families and salvage what remained of their weekend.

Lisa checked again that her slides were ready to go, knowing that she'd have the floor soon. She tucked a stray strand of hair behind her ear and smoothed her blouse.

"We also have an expert with us who can give us his insight into the situation," said Barry, nodding to Martin.

Lisa sensed Martin straightening in his seat beside her and noticed a subtle and silent snort from Christine.

"Firstly, I've been on calls with London regarding the investigation into the Solar Flare. The Prime Minister has activated a Cobra committee and they're coordinating the response. They're taking this threat very seriously," said Barry.

Martin huffed his disagreement. Lisa hoped no one else picked up on it.

"We've been instructed not to release any public statements at this time," Barry glanced at Lisa. He must've felt her disapproving look.

"It's expected that they'll make a nationwide public announcement later this evening," he continued.

Lisa could see Martin out of the corner of her eye. He was shaking his head, an outburst imminent.

"In the meantime, we have a Professor of Astrophysics from Queen's University with us," Barry paused and looked down at his notes, "Professor Martin Monroe. Thank you for coming in, Professor."

Martin nodded curtly.

Christine sat back in her seat, arms folded tightly across her chest, lips pursed and eyebrows as high as they could go on her forehead.

"Lisa, I believe you and the Professor have prepared some slides," said Barry.

"Yes, Barry, thank you," said Lisa.

She transferred her screen to the projector, which displayed a slide entitled *Implications of CME.*

Tapping the spacebar on her keyboard, she advanced to the next slide, which listed the *Immediate Effects.*

Lisa cleared her throat. She could feel a prickly heat rising on her neck and cheeks. She sat forward on the edge of her seat.

"Professor Monroe has been studying Solar Flares and Coronal Mass Ejections for the last ten years. The CME which occurred early this morning is the largest he has ever seen," said Lisa by way of introduction.

"It is actually the largest that has ever been recorded," said Martin, looking around the room and returning his gaze to Barry. "Nothing even remotely this big has ever been observed."

Lisa nodded at Martin and smiled. "The Professor has detailed some effects that we can expect when the CME reaches Earth later this evening," she continued.

"What time's it due to hit?" asked Danny.

"It's difficult to say exactly, but sometime in the next three to five hours," Martin replied sharply.

"Has anyone confirmed that?" asked Christine, without looking away from the projector screen, arms still folded.

Lisa looked at Martin, a little embarrassed that she hadn't asked that question during her review with him. *Please say they have*, she thought.

"Yes, over the past fourteen hours, the scientific community has been talking about nothing else," said Martin to the side of Christine's face. "The data has been checked and confirmed."

"Okay folks, let's hold off on the questions until the end please," said Barry. "Lisa, go ahead."

"These are the immediate effects that can be expected," said Lisa, lifting one hand away from her computer and gesturing at the list now displayed on the large screen.

"CMEs that have reached Earth in the past have affected power grids in a localised area.

Because of the size and speed of this CME, the affect will be much larger and will potentially cause damage to power grids on a global scale." Lisa turned to Martin to see if he'd anything to add. Martin nodded for her to continue.

The frown on Greg's face suggested he was more than a little sceptical of this fact, but he said nothing.

"Severe damage to the power grid infrastructure is expected," Lisa continued. "This will cause loss of power across the entire network."

"Again, because of the magnitude of the CME, the associated electromagnetic storm will cause catastrophic damage to transformers, relays, and other critical equipment," added Martin.

Some heads turned towards Martin, and some glanced at Greg to see his reaction.

"A more alarming issue is the potential risk to life caused by radiation exposure to air passengers travelling at high altitude," said Lisa, directing the comment again at Barry.

"The Cobra committee is taking advice on this and is considering grounding air traffic," said Barry in response to several quizzical looks from around the table. Even Christine turned in her seat to hear Barry's comment.

"When?" asked Martin. "It may already be too late. Most of the flights that'll be affected are already in the air," he said forcefully. "Are they going to instruct them all to land?"

"Something like that would take hours to coordinate," said the Transport liaison.

"I don't have an update on that, but my understanding is that it *is* in hand," said Barry, nodding for Lisa to continue.

Lisa continued through the points on her slides, talking about communications, banking, transport, lack of supplies in shops and the impact on emergency services. The occasional question came from the audience, but most held fire, as requested by Barry.

As the list went on, the sheer scale of the situation began to register on the faces in the room. There was horror and scepticism in equal measure.

"I'm just not getting it," said Danny in his deep breathy voice and with a disarming smile aimed at Lisa. "Okay there might be a power outage for a few hours or maybe one or two days, but surely the electric company will work around the clock to get it up and running again?" he looked to Greg for affirmation.

Greg nodded and shrugged slightly.

Lisa opened her mouth to answer, but Martin got in first.

"No, I'm sorry you're right, you're not getting it," snapped Martin, a little more aggressively than Lisa would've hoped.

"In normal circumstances, that would be the case. The power outage would be localised to a certain area, and therefore there wouldn't be such major disruption to communications. They could just phone and have spare parts delivered. They could call their engineers and have them come in." Martin paused for a breath but was by no means finished. Lisa feared a full-on rant was coming.

Danny listened politely, but his smile had faded.

"The problem here, is that those repairs will not be so easy," Martin continued. "There will be so much damage to infrastructure that there won't be enough replacement transformers or relays or other parts, and even if there was, they may not be able to communicate with the suppliers or arrange transportation." He started directing his response to others around the room, intent on getting his message to sink in. "And even if they could arrange transportation, how will the vehicles get fuel if all the petrol stations are out of action? How will repair teams fuel their vehicles? How will the company even get a hold of them to direct them to where the repairs are needed?"

Martin turned again to Danny. "You see, it is the sheer scale of the problem that makes this situation so serious."

Danny curled the edges of his mouth downward in contemplation and bobbed his head, accepting Martin's point, but not totally convinced.

Barry leaned forward on his elbows. "Greg, any thoughts? I mean, in terms of replacement parts and repair teams and that?"

"Well, I used to work as one of those repair engineers, so I have some experience in power cuts. Now, we *were* usually contacted via mobile when on call, so there might be some issues there," he said, nodding slightly to Martin. "I spoke to the Duty Incident Manager in NIE Networks this afternoon and they're aware that there may be some issues later, so they've already brought in extra teams, so I wouldn't worry too much about that."

Martin shook his head and sighed.

"In terms of replacement parts," said Greg, "it depends what failures they have. They will have certain replacements on hand. Larger transformers they'd need to get from the central warehouse."

"Do petrol stations not have generators?" asked an older lady at the end of the table. Lisa couldn't remember her name.

All eyes turned to the Transport liaison. "Ah, I don't know. I wouldn't think many would," she said, slightly taken off guard.

"What about the hospitals?" asked the same woman, turning to her neighbour who dealt with the emergency services.

"Yes, all the hospitals are equipped with generators to provide power during a power cut," he said without hesitation.

"And how long are those generators designed to work for?" asked Martin, setting up his next question.

"They can be used for as long as is needed," he replied, still confident.

"They run on diesel, right?" asked Martin.

"Yes."

"And where do they get their diesel from?" asked Martin rhetorically, exaggerating his point by turning his hands palms up.

The confident responses ceased.

Christine finally broke her silence with a deep sigh. "I'm sorry this just seems like scaremongering to me," she said, turning to Barry, although clearly intending the comments for Lisa and Martin.

"I mean, if it was this bad, would it not be on every news channel and would there not be public announcements already?" she said with a sneer.

"Who do you think puts out those announcements, Christine?" snapped Lisa. "We do. That's why we're here right now, trying to get the facts so we can inform the public."

"Okay folks, that's a lot of information and some good questions," Barry tried to take control of the conversation, when Christine continued.

"Barry, I don't think we should base our decisions on one opinion, particularly..." she paused and turned to Martin, "I'm sorry to say Professor but you do have a bit of a reputation for exaggeration." She tilted her head and smirked, then turned immediately to Barry.

"Excuse me?" said Martin.

"Should we worry about an alien spaceship coming with this solar flare?" she said, "Barry, this is ridiculous."

Martin fell quiet and dropped his head to study his phone.

"Christine, I don't know what your problem is," said Lisa, feeling the need to come to Martin's defence. "Professor Monroe has given up his time to come in here and help us understand what we're dealing with. I don't think it's too much to ask for us to keep an open mind, or at the very least, show some professional courtesy."

Lisa glared at Christine, unblinking, then turned her pointed glare to Barry, expecting some backup from him.

"If you don't believe what I'm telling you, Christine," said Martin, surprisingly calmly, Lisa thought, "then have a look at what's being said on this forum." He placed his phone on the table and slid it across towards Christine.

"Those are some of the most renowned and well-respected scientists on the planet," he said, sitting back and folding his arms. "If you don't believe what they are saying, then I can't help you."

"Look at the colour of the sky," said James, who was sitting directly opposite. He was staring over Lisa's shoulder and out through the window behind her.

All eyes focused on the windows. A noticeable green hue washed across the view.

"It's the Aurora Borealis," said Martin, as he reached across the table to retrieve his phone, he was done trying to convince these people. "This is the start of the electromagnetic storm."

As most of the team made their way to the windows, Martin gathered his belongings and headed for the door. "It won't be long now," he said to Barry as he passed.

Lisa stared questioningly at Barry.

"Barry, we need to put a statement out now," she said firmly. "Saying nothing is no longer an option."

"I need to get back on with London first. Draft something but don't release it until I give the go ahead. Everyone else, reach out to your contacts and find out if they're aware of the issue and if not let them know that guidance will be issued in the next couple of hours," said Barry, mostly to the backs of heads as they stared at the colouring sky outside.

Lisa closed her laptop and got up to follow Martin. Barry leaned in. "And try to get the Professor to stay, will you, Lisa? I think we're gonna need him."

Martin stood outside the main doors to the building. His breathing was still heavy, but the fluttering in his chest had started to subside.

He stared up at the blanket of colours being shaken out across the sky. He'd seen the

Aurora Borealis in person only once before, during a visit to Iceland. This display was already much more intense. It was beautiful, awe-inspiring, devastating.

Tearing his focus from the dancing sky, he looked down at his phone, which he clutched too tightly in his hand. He wanted to call Simon, just to hear a friendly voice, someone who knew the truth, someone who believed him. He needed Simon.

The reflection of the sky played across his phone like a holographic screen saver. He pressed the speed dial icon saved on this home page.

"Hi Simon," said Martin, the despondency in his voice hard to hide.

"*Hey Prof*," said Simon, "how's it going there?"

"Yeah, okay."

"You sure? You sound off," said Simon. "I mean, apart from the world about to end, what's up?"

"Don't joke, Simon. I thought these people were starting to take this seriously, but no one seems able to make a decision."

"What are they saying?"

"Not much at all. A Cobra committee has been called in London, but they haven't even made a public announcement yet."

"Seriously? Do they not believe the data?"

"I don't know. All they're saying is that they're taking advice and considering the options," said Martin with a deep sigh.

"And what are the ones here saying?"

"Same really. I outlined the facts and the potential consequences, but..." he tailed off.

"Do they not accept it?" asked Simon.

"I think it's me they don't accept."

"What do you mean?"

"One of them brought up the Hale-Bopp thing," said Martin. Just saying the words brought a lump to his throat. He didn't want to go back to those dark days.

"You know what mate, fuck 'em. If they don't want to listen, then just tell them to go fuck themselves," fumed Simon. "Come round here, stay with me and we'll go to Fermanagh in the morning."

Martin could think of nothing better.

"You know what, I might just do that," said Martin, feeling a little better at the suggestion.

"I assume you've seen the light-show?" asked Simon.

"Yeah, and this's just the start of it. It's going to get a lot more intense."

"Well, I'm out on my balcony with a glass of wine. Come on over."

"Okay, I will. See you soon," said Martin, decision made. He owed these people nothing.

The weight of responsibility lifted from him and he took a deep breath, the first relaxed breath he'd taken since he'd woken that morning.

He heard his name being called, and the anxiety flooded back.

"Martin," said Lisa. He hadn't heard her come out behind him.

He looked at her sternly, then looked away.

"Look, I'm sorry Martin. Christine was out of order. She's a difficult character at the best of times and obviously some people handle crises better than others."

Martin was silent and continued to follow the waves of light across the sky.

"You know what? Fuck that, she's just a bitch," said Lisa, breaking the silence.

Martin turned and regarded her for a second, then smiled.

"I think I'm going to go, Lisa," he said. "I've told you all I can. What you do with that information is up to you now."

"Please Martin, we still need your help. I believe what you're saying, and I know a lot of the others are starting to realise how big this is, too."

"You don't need me. Sure, the decisions are being made in London, anyway."

"Or not being made, as it would seem," said Lisa, raising an eyebrow.

"They've bigger experts than me advising them."

"But we need to coordinate things locally. We really do need your help, Martin, please."

"What else can *I* do?"

"Once we get the go ahead from London, I'll be drafting local announcements and the rest of the team will be advising their various areas," she said. "No one here knows more about this than you."

"I don't know."

"And I'll make sure you get on the TV news and get listened too."

"Once the power goes off, which will be soon," he said, opening his hands and gesturing to the sky, "TV news will be pointless. Even if they're still able to broadcast, no one will see it."

"Yeah, of course," said Lisa. "Well then, radio news, we'll get you on every radio station that's still transmitting."

Martin looked at her. She couldn't have known how badly things had gone for him the last time he did a radio interview, or she wouldn't have used that as an argument.

They stood side by side in silence and starred in awe at the mesmerising orchestra of colours.

Martin could think of no better way to spend this last normal night than with his only friend Simon, but he knew he could be of some help here. He'd spent the last decade studying these phenomena. He knew what to expect. *What was the point of all that work and all that knowledge if I don't make use of it in a situation like this?* he thought.

"It's amazing, isn't it?" said Lisa, breaking the silence.

"It is."

"Martin, I need to go back in and start drafting a public announcement for when we get the green light." She looked up as a wave of green illuminated the broken clouds. "Excuse the pun," she added with a smile.

Martin smiled and shook his head.

"Will you help me?" she asked again.

CHAPTER 10

The muffled calls of the coxswain were all the distraction needed to steal Simon's attention from his new book, which hadn't quite gripped him yet.

The thin nine-man training boat glided past under his large circular window, as they did most evenings. With the armchair pulled close and his feet on the low windowsill, the small alcove off the living room was the perfect reading spot.

He wasn't normally so easily distracted, but tomorrow would've been Sarah's birthday and it was all he could think about. But she was gone, taken, along with their dreams. He longed to have dreams again.

Simon bathed in the warm glow from the retreating sun as he gazed out at the river.

Something was different, the colour was wrong. He craned his neck and looked up at the sky.

The Northern Lights, he thought. This must be the start of it.

He put his book on the windowsill and lifted his wine. As he moved through to the front of the apartment for a better view from his balcony, his phone rang.

He felt better after the short call with Martin. The professor wasn't in great form either, so the fact that he was coming over would likely be good for them both.

He rested his elbows on the metal railing that topped the wall of his small parapet balcony overlooking the front of the complex. He'd be able to see Martin when he arrived and could open the gate from there with his remote control. From five floors up, he'd a decent view of the city.

For the past couple of months Simon's routine, on most evenings, had been to pour a glass of red wine and stand on the balcony to watch one of the most breath-taking spectacles he'd ever seen, a Murmuration of starlings performing aerial stunts in their tens, if not hundreds, of thousands.

Each night, as soon as the light started to fade, the secret call would go out and a multitude of individual flocks would rendezvous above their roosting spots in the eaves of the bridges spanning the river. The gathering would grow into a cloud of small birds, wheeling and turning in hypnotic unison like a column of smoke being tossed by the wind.

As a boy, Simon remembered being left awe-struck on the rare occasion that he'd see the magical sight.

Now it was a nightly occurrence, and he'd a front-row seat. He sometimes felt like he was in the middle of the performance, when the birds, as if navigating with a single mind, would whoosh low over the roof of his building only feet above his head. The sounds of their wings and high-pitched chirps were deafening and exhilarating.

Thankfully, they'd never carpet-bombed him, while he stood gawking upwards, or his wine, and likely his evening, would've been ruined.

Sarah would have loved this view, he thought with a sip of his wine and a soul-deep sigh.

Tonight, though, there wasn't a bird in the sky, nor a single chirp. Instead, the sky was filled with a different captivating sight, a light show to top all others.

The rolling waves of colours bathed the streets and buildings with slowly changing mood lighting; green and purple and blue.

From his vantage point, he could see he wasn't the only spectator. Below, in the carpark, he could see some of his neighbours standing by their cars staring, open-mouthed, at the frolicking lights.

Some turned in slow circles, taking in the full extent of the scene.

Eugene, from the second floor, caught his eye as he panned around and waved up. Simon returned the gesture, more of a lazy salute than a wave.

Across the street a silent, three-man rave had started. Outside the front doors of the four-story social housing block directly opposite, three figures swayed and bobbed as if in time with three different pieces of dance music.

Completely off their trolleys, Simon thought.

One shuffled perilously close to the curb and was half a turn from stumbling out into the busy junction. His knee-length, green parka hung loosely on his tall, thin frame.

His two dance partners were shirtless. Both as skinny as their friend, but one had an unusually large head which wobbled as he moved. They stretched their arms high to the lights, which likely created an augmented reality for their substance fuelled hallucinations.

Simon was confident, given that they lived in Heroin Heights, that they were indeed on some mind-altering drugs which the Aurora Borealis was now enhancing.

It was a police officer who'd first referred to the apartment block by this unenviable title. Unofficially, of course.

Simon had been giving a statement about some stolen bikes and the cop, speaking more candidly than he probably should, told him about the ongoing trouble they were having with the residents of the building.

"Mostly heroin addicts and sex offenders with nowhere else to go," the officer had said.

The perfect neighbours for a two grand a month luxury apartment complex, Simon had thought at the time.

But Simon had only three months left on his lease and would soon be back in Southampton, near his mother and sister, so it didn't bother him that much.

For now, the three ravers seemed harmless enough, although he'd seen them in the past, in less jovial form.

He'd walked past the front of their building once or twice when they were loitering, either unable to score or between doses of prescribed methadone. He remembered the unease he felt when their searching, red-rimmed eyes locked on to him as he approached. He'd taken the basic precautions of stowing his phone and making sure his hands were free, just in case. Perhaps a more prudent approach would've been to cross to the other side of the road and give them a wide berth. But pride trumped prudence.

That was even after he'd watched, on another night, as it took four cops to subdue the tall guy after he'd kicked off in the middle of the street. So maybe it was stupidity that trumped prudence.

But tonight, they seemed harmless. He smiled as they continued their salutation to the sky.

The stem of his wineglass pinged off the metal railing as he lifted it to take a drink. Simon's heart skipped a beat as he realised he'd nearly lost it over the side. Leaning out, he looked down to see what damage he would've caused had it dropped. The bonnet of a red BMW would've been the bullseye.

In addition to the impromptu rave at the front doors, Heroin Heights was a hive of activity as various residents enjoyed the show from their apartments. Either through twitching curtains or by hanging precariously from wide-open windows.

Simon shuddered to think how these poor souls would cope if the power was off for an extended period. He imagined most were on their own, likely estranged from their families for various reasons.

He took another sip of his wine and pulled his phone from his pocket. He was just about to dial his sister when a text arrived from Martin.

Sorry Simon, going to stay here and help. Will come and get you when I'm done.

Simon pursed his lips and shook his head slowly. He dialled his sister.

"Hi Sam."

"Hey, twice in one day, that's a first," said his older sister Samantha.

"Did you go out and get fuel and provisions, like I said?" asked Simon.

"Yes,"

"Both cars?"

"Yes," said Samantha, a hint of irritation in her voice. "I'll tell you, you're not Pete's favourite person right now. I made him go out and do his car during half time in the match and by the time he got back he'd missed the United goal."

"Well, he'll thank me later in the week when he can still use his car."

"You really think it's gonna be that bad?"

"I don't know, but Martin does, and he's the expert," said Simon. "Did you call in to mum's?"

"Yeah, not long back."

"Did she get stuff in like I told her?"

"She says she's got plenty."

"Jesus, Sam. Can you call her and get her to go out and stock up?"

"You know what she's like Simon, anyway her larder would last her two months at least," said Samantha.

"Okay, look, Martin says the power's gonna go off pretty soon, so just make sure you have candles or torches or whatever, close at hand."

"Yes, I have them set out. If this turns out to be bullshit though, you'll be buying this mountain of candles off me," she said with a laugh.

"Some chance," said Simon with a snort. "Tell me, do you have a landline phone?"

"No, haven't had a landline in years. Why?"

"Mobiles probably aren't gonna work for a while."

"You think so?"

"Yes, so if I don't get talking to you for a while, stay safe and keep an eye on mum."

"Will do. You too."

"Okay, I'll go and phone mum again. Chat soon. Bye."

"Bye Simon."

Simon called his mother and tried to scold her for not following his advice from earlier. She convinced him that she had everything she'd need, and for him not to worry. The tables were then reversed, and he had to recant all the preparations he'd made for the power cut.

"Are you sure that friend of yours knows what he's talking about?" she asked.

"Yes, he knows his stuff," said Simon.

"He's a bit of a strange fella, isn't he?" said his mum. She'd only met Martin once, at Sarah's funeral.

"He's a bit eccentric, but he's a good guy," said Simon.

The conversation then drifted from the imminent power cut to a soap opera style summary of her neighbours' lives. Deaths, births and marriages.

Simon was close to regretting making the call when his mum suddenly realised that her favourite *actual* soap opera was about to start on TV. They instructed each other to stay safe, and he promised to call again as soon as he could.

In the brief time that he'd been on the phone, Simon could see that a couple more parties had started in the apartment block opposite. Lights blazed in several windows and competing bass tones spilt out into the street.

Kaleidoscope skies, what better excuse for a party, he thought.

If Martin was right, then this might be their last chance to party for a while. Simon stepped back inside and pulled the sliding patio door behind him.

CHAPTER 11

Martin dreaded the thought of going back into the conference room. It'd been years since anyone had mentioned the Hale-Bopp episode. It'd taken so long for people to forget about it, and even longer for Martin to get over the impact it had on him mentally. He was on that roller coaster of emotions again. The cycle of anger, frustration, and embarrassment was exhausting. He just wanted to curl up in a ball as he'd done so many times before.

"Let's go in here again," said Lisa, directing him into the interview room they'd first used. He nodded, afraid the relief would be audible if he spoke. Then came the inevitable question. "So do you mind me asking what Christine's comment was about?" asked Lisa, a hint of caution in her voice and more than a hint of contempt for Christine.

Martin closed his eyes and let out a long breath. He wished he'd just left and gone to Simon's. But Lisa seemed to be on his side. She seemed to understand the gravity of what he'd told her. Was her trust about to evaporate? Was she going to see him as a hysterical nut, like everyone else had? What was the point of him being here? He could just get up and leave now. *Simon was right. He owed these people nothing,* he thought.

He let out a long sigh, "Okay look, she was talking about a radio interview I did a long time ago..."

Lisa listened patiently as Martin gave her the details. He surprised himself with his ability to remain composed as he relayed his very public and undeserved fall from grace. Her sympathetic expression helped. Although he wasn't about to reveal the extent of the

emotional toll, the whole episode had taken on
him. She was a stranger. Outside of his family,
Simon was the only person who knew the full
story.

"That's awful, Martin," said Lisa, genuine
sympathy in her voice. "Was there nothing you
could do legally against the reporter or the
radio station?"

Martin sucked his cheeks and shook his head.
"I was advised that it would just add fuel to the
fire, and I might not even be able to prove that
he doctored the recording."

"That's crazy."

Martin nodded and shuffled his paperwork,
just for something to do with his hands.

"I suppose it doesn't help when people like
Christine bring it up again."

"No, it doesn't, especially when she should be
focusing on more important issues. Some
people just hear gossip and form an opinion."

"Well, all you can do is keep pointing out the facts. You can't force people to believe you… I believe you."

Martin smiled, "Thank you, Lisa." It was strange how hearing that, from just one person, lifted his spirits.

"Anyway, once we get the go ahead, I will be the one communicating the message to the public, well locally anyway."

"Okay, good," said Martin.

Lisa opened her laptop. "Let's start drafting an announcement for when we do get the green light."

Martin and Lisa were working on the wording of the public announcement when a message from Barry came with a ping.

"Barry's called us all to the conference room again. He must have news," said Lisa, standing and beckoning for Martin to join her.

Barry was already in the conference room when they arrived. He looked flustered and impatient. When the room filled, he informed the waiting audience that the Cobra committee had increased the severity level of the threat and was now taking action to alert the public. They'd instructed the Civil Aviation Authority to ground all flights until further notice, as had other countries.

"The Prime Minister is due to address the country soon," said Barry.

Martin was relieved, but he couldn't help thinking that it was too little, too late. People wouldn't have time to prepare, particularly this late on a Sunday night. He looked across the table at Christine. The changing colours from the windows behind him had intensified and played across her face. She avoided eye contact.

"Lisa, have you prepared a statement?" Barry asked.

"Yes, I have a draft with the key facts but we'll need to follow up with practical advice about emergency services etc," said Lisa.

"Okay, good," said Barry, turning to the liaison for the emergency services. "Leon, can you work with Lisa on those details please?"

Barry didn't wait for an answer. "We'll also need a comment from the electricity company on likely down time," he said, switching his attention to Greg.

"They'll not know that until they know what the damage is," said Greg, a slight twist of his face betraying a hint of attitude.

"Okay, as soon as they know, we'll need to get that information out," said Barry, moving to his next point with urgency. "Danny, any word from the Army? Have they been given any orders yet?"

Danny sat forward, but before he could respond, the florescent lights above the table flickered, clicked, and went dark.

A chorus of murmurs rose around the table. The only illumination in the room was from the pale glow of the inhabitants' laptop screens and the ominous wash of colour from the windows. Martin looked at his watch. It was 10.20pm.

"For God's sake!" Barry checked his phone. "Does anyone have a signal?"

Martin looked at the signal indicator on his own phone. Nothing.

"I've four bars," said Christine, flashing the screen to Barry. "No, hold on," she added, rechecking. "No, it's gone."

The rest of the room reported the same.

It was now Martin who resisted making eye contact with Christine. He didn't trust himself not to have an '*I told you so*' expression on his face.

Barry continued with instructions and the group broke up, each going in search of a landline phone to try to get in touch with their various contacts.

Lisa and Martin stood with Barry under the pale glow of an emergency light in the hallway and reviewed the draft announcement. He agreed with the wording and asked Lisa to start calling the radio stations to instruct them to broadcast the message.

"I need to try to contact the SAGE team in London and see what the plan is," said Barry. "Let me know how you get on with the radio stations."

On the way to Lisa's office, they took a slight detour and stepped outside. The sky was even more vibrant than before, with the light pollution from the city now almost completely gone. The streetlights and the limited number of buildings, visible from their vantage point, were in complete darkness. The only artificial light came from the sparse traffic that passed by the gates.

"Are you still okay to stay and help Martin?" asked Lisa. "They've rooms set up with bunks. They're not great, but they'll do the job."

"Yes, that's fine, I can stay," said Martin.

"Okay, let's phone this announcement through to the radio stations. I've a landline at my desk."

Lisa sat at her desk and Martin pulled a chair up next to her. She opened her laptop, which was now on 70% battery. *I should've printed these numbers earlier*, she thought, as she opened a file with the telephone numbers for local television and radio stations.

"We've got a problem," said Martin, lifting the receiver of the phone sitting on the desk. "This phone won't work. We need a non-electronic landline phone." He held the receiver to his ear and shook his head, confirming that there was no dial tone.

"Shit, I hadn't realised that was also plugged into the power," said Lisa, as she got up and walked around the room to confirm what she already suspected, that all the other phones were the same as hers.

"I might know where there's one," she said. "Would you mind writing out the contact details from that file please, while I go and try to find one?"

Lisa went to a small storage room in the hall. She'd remember coming across a box previously which, if she remembered correctly, was filled with a jumble of old phones. *Hopefully, they were the type that didn't need a separate power supply*, she thought.

She retrieved the box from the bottom shelf at the back of the room and untangled one of the phones. She was relieved to see that it only had one wire protruding from the back, and it had the small square phone jack connector on the end.

As she carried the box back to her office, she met other members of the team, all with the same issue. She felt like Santa as she handed out the precious gifts, making sure to keep one for herself.

Back at her desk, she ducked under and plugged the phone into the socket. As she rose again, she saw Martin with the receiver to his ear shaking his head again.

"Shit," she spat as she slumped into her chair, her elation at having found the phones evaporated.

Martin looked around the room. "Is that printer also a fax machine?" he asked, pointing at the large multipurpose machine in the corner.

"Yes."

"It might have a dedicated outside line," said Martin.

Lisa unplugged the phone again and with help from Martin she edged the heavy printer out from the wall, exposing the socket behind. Holding the receiver to her ear, she connected the phone and looked at Martin with a smile.

She listened to the welcome hum of a dial tone before trying the first number on the list. The ringing tone repeated for longer than it should need to. No one was answering. She tried the next. Martin sat patiently, holding his mobile phone, with the torch app enabled, to help illuminate the darkening room. Again, the phone rang without answer. She looked at Martin and shook her head.

"They probably have the same problem, electronic switchboard," he said, frowning.

Lisa tried the next three numbers on the list. Finally, someone answered. She confirmed that they were still able to broadcast and then explained who she was and that she'd an official public announcement which needed to be aired immediately. She dictated the announcement to the radio station employee, who seemed a little hesitant.

"I'll have to check this with the producer," said the young voice on the end of the line.

"Is your producer there? Put them on the phone please," said Lisa.

"He's not here at the minute. I'll need to call him."

"Do you have a landline number for him?"

"Ah, no, just a mobile. Why?"

"Maybe you haven't noticed, but all the mobile networks are down, so how do you intend on getting him?"

"Oh right, of course. Look, I'm only a junior producer for the evening slot, I don't have the authority to put out public announcements. Can this wait until the morning?"

"No, it can't wait until the morning. This needs to go out straight away. This is a public emergency."

"Ah, can you hold on for a minute, please?"

There was silence on the phone. Lisa turned to Martin, who could hear the muffled responses of the radio station employee. He rolled his eyes.

"Hello," said a different voice on the line. "This is Andrew Jenkins. I'm the presenter of the evening show."

His voice was confident and clear, and Lisa could almost hear his polished smile.

"Hello Andrew, has your colleague explained the situation?"

"Yes, Miss Keenan, he has, but, as I'm sure you'll understand, we've protocols and procedures that we must follow. Unfortunately, we can't just put out an announcement without clearance," he said. "I mean, you could be anyone. You have to appreciate that we get a lot of prank calls."

"This is not a prank call, sir," said Lisa, raising her voice in frustration.

"Ask them how long they have generator power for," said Martin.

"I assume you're running on generator power. Is that correct?"

"Yes."

"How long will that generator last?"

"I'm sorry, I can't give out that information."

Martin slumped back in his chair.

"Okay, so you won't put the announcement out without clearance, and you can't get through to your senior producer to get clearance, is that right?" asked Lisa.

"I'm afraid so."

Lisa was losing her temper. "Mr Jenkins, I'll be at your door within the next thirty minutes. If I present you with my government identification, will that suffice? Let me be very clear, Mr Jenkins. If your answer is anything but yes, then I will be accompanied by the police and we will take control of your station under the Civil Contingencies Act. Do you understand?"

There was another period of silence on the line before the DJ responded in a slightly less confident voice, "Ah, yes, absolutely. If you can provide identification, then we'll be very happy to broadcast the announcement."

"Thank you. I'll see you in thirty minutes. Obviously, I won't be able to call you when I get there, so please have someone meet us at the door," said Lisa, riding high on her newfound authority.

Lisa hung up the phone without another word, blew out a long slow breath and turned to Martin with a schoolgirl grin.

Martin tilted his head and furrowed his brow. "Was that a bluff? Can you not take over the station if you need to?"

"I have no idea Martin," she stood, now nervously laughing. "I don't even know if there's anything to do with radio in the Civil

Contingencies Act, but thankfully neither did he."

Martin smiled and bobbed his head. He seemed impressed with the ballsy move. So was she.

"Right, let's go. We can call into the other local stations too."

CHAPTER 12

The oscillating whine of sirens drowned out the cries and shouts of the bystanders. The blue lights pulsed, and even with his eyes closed, they dazzled him.

At full stretch, all he could reach was her lifeless hand. He couldn't let go.

Strong hands wrestled him away. "Sir, we need to let the paramedics in there."

"That's my wife."

"Let them get to her," said the police officer, as he eased Simon away from the broken window. The neon green swarm of starlings drifted above his head, bright and brilliant. Now purple and blue.

"You have to help her," his anguish choked him as he watched helplessly. The cloud of birds, blue and green, swirled around him.

"They'll get through to her," said the officer. "What's your name, sir?"

"Simon. That's my wife."

"Okay, Simon, let's stand back here and give them space."

The driver of the lorry sat across the street, wrapped in his shame and a silver blanket. It shimmered blue and green. Beside him, two thin, bare-chested figures danced and laughed. Simon wanted to kill them all.

"She's dead. Isn't she?" he looked the young police officer in the eyes. The expression confirmed what he'd known for some time. She was gone.

"Help, can somebody help..." A whispered cry on the wind, unheard by all but him.

"She's alive," he pushed against the police officer, who held him tightly in a comforting, restraining embrace.

"Let me go, I heard her. She's alive."

The surrounding grip tightened. "Simon, she's gone. I'm sorry."

"We're stuck, somebody help..."

He woke with a start, confused and sweating. He looked at his alarm clock by the bed; it was blank. It took him a second to spool up and remember the power cut. It must've happened after he'd gone to bed. He squinted at his watch in the pale green light that bled through the curtains. The Aurora Borealis, he remembered. It was 2.30am.

Another dream. He hadn't had one in a while. At least it was early, five more hours of sleep, hopefully. He attacked his memory-foam pillow with punches and slaps and flipped it over for the soothing coolness.

He heard a thump. Or did he? Craning his head, he held his breath, focusing his ears. *If there's a follow-up in the next ten seconds I'll get up and check it, otherwise back to sleep,* he thought.

Hearing no other sounds, he let his head relax into the cool fresh pillow and hoped for less disturbing dreams.

###

Lisa woke early, as she usually did when she wasn't in her own bed. William, the janitor, had obviously been able to get the generator going, as the small room was uncomfortably warm and dry. Even from across the room, she could feel the heat emanating from the electric blow heater mounted on the wall.

The room was one of two that William had converted into temporary sleeping quarters the day before. One for males, the other for females. The conversion involved the removal of the conference table and the setup of two rows of camp beds. Not the most comfortable accommodation.

Out of the five females on the team, Lisa was the only one to spent the night in the makeshift accommodation, as had Martin. They hadn't returned from doing the rounds of the radio stations until after 1am.

The plan, if she could call it a plan, was to have a review meeting at 8am and then provide an updated statement to the radio stations. She was also hoping to get Martin to do a couple of interviews at the stations to help build some confidence.

Lisa carried her small overnight bag to the toilets across the hall. A shower room had been installed for use by the STAC team and, more so by employees who cycled to work or used the on-site gym at lunchtime. *It certainly beats doing a rub down with baby wipes,* Lisa thought.

Martin and Danny were sitting at one of the long tables in the kitchen when Lisa entered. The welcome smell of coffee filled the room.

"Good morning," said Danny theatrically. "Hope you had a comfortable night, madam."

Lisa smiled, "Morning," she said, heading for the kettle. "Wasn't too bad, although I wouldn't be a huge fan of those camp beds."

"Morning Lisa," said Martin quietly over his coffee mug.

She made herself a cup of instant coffee and sat beside Martin. "Did you stay here last night too, Danny?"

"Yeah, I was on and off with the Army most of the evening, trying to get an idea of their plans."

"And what are they saying?" said Lisa.

Martin huffed, obviously having already heard Danny's update and been less than impressed.

"Well, they haven't been given any specific orders yet," said Danny. "They've been told to standby in case they're required to assist in the coming days."

"They still think this is going to be fixed in a couple of days," fumed Martin. "It's not!"

"Don't shoot the messenger," said Danny with a shrug.

"How many soldiers are there here at the minute, anyway?" asked Lisa.

"Well, technically there's supposed to be about 4000 including the Army Reserve," said Danny, "but only about ten percent of the reserves are active at any one time so I'd say there's only about 2000 actually available, in total."

"We were just talking about this," said Martin, turning his chair slightly so he faced Lisa. "Most, if not all, of the shops are closed. Any that are open will only be able to take cash, right?"

"Okay," said Lisa.

Martin turned to Danny. "So what happens when people run out of cash? And remember, bank machines aren't working either."

Danny chewed on the inside of his lip and nodded.

"People still need to eat, so if the shops won't sell them anything, they're going to have to get it from somewhere," continued Martin.

"They'll loot," said Lisa.

"Well, if they don't get food and essentials from somewhere, then yes, looting will start," said Martin, raising his eyebrows at Lisa.

He turned to Danny again. "So the army will be needed either way, either to distribute food and water rations or to control the streets."

"Well, let's hope it doesn't get to that stage," said Danny.

"That's the thing. How long do you think the power will have to be off for before it does? A day? Two days? A week?" said Martin. His volume and pitch were starting to rise. *And rightly so,* thought Lisa.

"Imagine you're a parent with a young family… do you have a family Danny?" asked Martin, checking before he continued.

"Nope, just me," said Danny.

"Well, imagine you've a young family to feed, and you only have a few things in the cupboard; a half a litre of milk, some cereal, a loaf of bread and maybe a tin of spam that's been hiding way at the back," said Martin, taking a breath and noticing that Greg had joined them.

"Well, that stuff's only going to last a day or two. What would you do if the shops were closed or if you couldn't get cash for those that were open? Are you going to let your family go hungry? What if you've a baby and need baby food? How long will you wait before you kick a door down to get it?" He looked up at Greg and shrugged, as if inviting him to comment.

"Well, let's hope it doesn't come to that, and they can get it up and running again soon," said Danny.

Martin sat back and shook his head.

"Does the army have access to emergency rations or something, Danny? Or would they requisition food from warehouses and distribute it?" asked Lisa.

"I'm not sure about emergency rations, but yeah, they could take control of warehouses, I suppose, if they needed to," said Danny, leaning back and folding his arms. "But man-power would be the big problem. As I said, there's only about 2000 active personnel to cover the whole country."

"What's the word from the electric company?" asked Danny, turning to Greg.

"Not sure yet. I couldn't get through to them last night," said Greg. "I'm gonna try to get an update now." He headed off to find one of the working phones.

CHAPTER 13

Simon blinked and stared blankly at the dull face of his digital alarm clock. Gradually, the world around him resolved. He stretched out the muscles of his arms and legs, readying them for the day. Still groggy, he rolled to sit on the edge of the bed. There was a chill in the air. *Of course, the heating's off,* he thought.

He scrambled into his clothes, keen to keep the morning chill off his skin, and plodded through to the kitchen in his sock-soles. He'd never owned a pair of house slippers, but he'd welcome them now for the cold wooden floors. A quick glance confirmed that the electricity was still off. There was no life in any of the small LEDs, on the many devices in the living room and kitchen.

Leaning over the sink, he gazed out the window at the apartments across the river. The bright morning view gave no evidence of a power cut, but why would it? The small sliver of road that he could see from that angle showed the occasional vehicle, but it was still early.

He looked at his desk and workstation. The Markets would be closed today, so nothing for him to do work-wise. The financial impact of a power outage, even for just a couple of days, would be huge. Hundreds of millions would be wiped off certain stocks. If he'd have known about the coming events on Friday, he could've placed some extremely profitable shorts. *You callous, capitalist bastard*, he thought.

He wondered how Martin was getting on and checked his phone. No signal. He had everything he needed for the trip ready to go for when Martin arrived, except some foodstuff which he'd throw in a box.

Simon looked around the kitchen, still sleepy. He relied on his morning coffee to kick-start him for the day. Twisting the knob, he tried the gas on the stove. He could boil the water in a saucepan. There was a short hiss from the nozzle and then nothing. He frowned and cursed.

He remembered the small camping stove that'd been packed away with his tent and sleeping bags. It was now in a box, ready for the trip to Martin's place. He could use that.

The cardboard box of stuff, which Simon thought would be useful to bring on his exodus from the city, sat in the hall beside the front door. As he stooped over it to retrieve the small gas cooker, he heard a faint banging. It obviously wasn't on his door, more likely an apartment lower down. He unlocked his door and peered out into the gloomy hall.

He listened for a moment, and just as he started to close the door, he heard it again. A thud, thud, thud on a metallic surface. Then a muffled voice, "Somebody help, help us, we're stuck." It was a high-pitched female voice, urgent and desperate.

He stepped out into the hall and leaned over the stairwell balcony. It came again from behind him. He turned and immediately realised where the cry for help was coming from. The elevator. It must be stuck between floors.

He approached the doors of the elevator. "Hello, is someone in there?"

"Yes, help us, we're stuck, we need help, please help. My granny isn't well. Get help quick," came the female voice with a mix of relief and panic.

"Okay, stay there, I'll get help," he shouted into the crack in the doors. *Stay there? Where're they* gonna *go, you idiot?* he thought. He looked back to his apartment briefly in a moment of indecision, then moved to the door across the hall. He hesitated, fist hovering in front of Mrs Flemming's door. *It must be Janet and one of her grand-daughters*, he thought.

He banged hard on the door anyway, just in case his assumption was wrong, and then bounded down the stairs to the next level without waiting for an answer. He needed help; he didn't have a landline phone; he needed to find someone who did.

He thumped urgently on the first door and then immediately strode to the opposite apartment and repeated the rude summons for attention. He moved impatiently to the top of the stairs again, focus moving between the two doors. With no sound of approaching occupants, he jumped down to the next floor, steadying himself on the handrail. If someone above did answer, they'd hear him below.

He banged again on the two doors on the third floor and started shouting for help. A door above clicked open, and a face appeared, leaning over the banister, just as one of the doors he'd just knocked also opened.

An agitated, bleary-eyed man peered out from behind a half-open door.

"What's going on?" came the voice from above.

"There's someone stuck in the lift," said Simon unapologetically. "Do either of you have a landline phone?" He looked between the face above and the man who'd now stepped out into the hall beside him.

"There's a power cut. My mobile isn't working. We need to phone the fire service. Do you have a landline?" he said, the urgency rising in his voice.

"No," said the voice from above, looking behind him towards the elevator. "What floor are they on?"

"Between four and five, I think," said Simon.

He turned again to the man standing beside him. "Do you have a landline phone?"

"No, just a mobile. Hold on," he said as he ducked back inside. He reappeared a few seconds later, mobile phone in hand. He shook his head. "I've no signal."

"Neither have I. I think they're all gonna be down. We need to find a landline," repeated Simon, already halfway down to the next floor. "Can you go up and let them know we're trying to get help?"

"Okay."

Simon banged again, even louder, on the two doors on the second floor and, without stopping, descended to the first floor to repeat the action. He heard a door open on the floor above and met the familiar face of Eugene — an electrician, ironically — as he climbed the stairs again.

"Simon, what's going on?" said Eugene.

"Eugene, do you have a landline phone?" asked Simon, joining him on the second floor landing. "There's someone trapped in the lift. I think it's Mrs Flemming and her granddaughter. They must've been in there all night. There's a power cut."

"Shit. Yeah, I saw that the power was off. I was just about to check my fuses. I thought it might've been just my apartment," said Eugene.

"No, it's everywhere, and all the mobiles are down."

"That's strange. No, I don't have a landline," said Eugene, as he confirmed that his mobile phone was also unusable.

"Do you know how to get the elevator doors open?" asked Simon.

"I'm not sure. I think there's a manual release somewhere."

Simon and Eugene hurried up the stairs and joined a small, but growing, group of neighbours on the fourth floor. One man who'd been communicating with the trapped girl turned from the doors of the elevator. "It's definitely between four and five," he said. "The girl says her granny's unconscious."

Eugene edged past the group to examine the elevator doors.

"I can't find anyone with a landline," said Simon. He stepped up beside Eugene. "Do you think you can get it open?"

"I'm not sure."

"I tried forcing it, but it won't budge," said the man from the third floor.

"No, there's a safety mechanism on lifts now. You can't force them open," said Eugene. He ran his finger over a small hole about six inches from the top of the door. "But I think this's the release if we can get something to fit it."

"Like a screwdriver?" asked one of the neighbours.

"Might work. I'll be back in a second," said Eugene, already heading for the stairs.

Simon turned to the others on the landing. "We should keep looking for someone with a landline."

"I'll go and check the other apartments," said the man from the third floor. His neighbour followed him.

Simon leaned in and put his ear close to the door. He could hear sobbing.

"Hello," he shouted. "We're going to try to get the doors open."

"Please help my granny," the young girl cried back. "I think she's stopped breathing."

Simon heard the clatter of Eugene's toolbox as he appeared at his side.

"She says her granny has stopped breathing," said Simon.

"Fuck! Any word on a phone?"

"No, not yet."

"Let me in there," said Eugene, producing a long thin sliver of metal. Simon stepped to the side.

Eugene pushed the thin rod into the small hole in the elevator door. "Try to pull the doors back when I say."

Simon squeezed in beside Eugene and gripped the edge of the door. He doubted he could apply much force with only his fingertips getting purchase. He heard a click from where the rod was inserted and immediately felt the tension on the door release slightly. It started to ease back and, as Eugene added his hands, Simon was able to reposition and get a full grip on the door. Between the two of them, they managed to slide the door across into its recess in the wall.

With the door now open, Simon found himself with his toes right on the edge of the lift shaft. The cold blackness swept across his face as he peered down into the void. He felt an invisible force beckoning him forward. He took a step back, edging Eugene away.

At the top of the opening, the bottom of the lift car was visible, but only about ten inches of the internal doors were in view. They'd need to go up to the fifth floor and do the same there.

After a slightly easier wrestle with the door on the upper floor, Simon and Eugene were presented with a slightly bigger portion of the elevator car. They could now see the top of the car and about eighteen inches of the door.

The door had a hydraulic arm attached at the top, which was locking it in the closed position. Eugene knelt and studied the mechanism closely while rubbing at the back of his neck. From Simon's point of view, the mechanism was just a random jumble of levers, hoses and wires. He was thankful that Eugene seemed a bit more clued in on the anatomy of the device.

With a twist of a heavy-duty screwdriver, Eugene pried a catch from the arm and the door eased open a fraction of an inch. As the two men strained to pull the doors apart, a wave of stale air rose from the car and the face of the young captive appeared in the opening.

Her bloodshot eyes and wet cheeks betrayed the terrifying night that she and her grandmother had spent in the cramped, pitch-black box. Simon felt a chill on his spine as the teenager placed her hands on the ledge, her fingers spanning the opening between the elevator and the landing floor.

The entrance to an elevator had always been a source of anxiety for Simon. Since childhood, he'd had an irrational fear of the lift moving just as he was halfway in. Even to this day, he would quick-step through the door just in case. He imagined now, the braking mechanism giving way and the elevator slicing the girl's fingers off or worse, slicing her in half as she climbed out.

Climbing out might not be an option in this case, though. The opening seemed too narrow. Simon looked down into the space. The light from the stairwell window did little to help illuminate the elevator, but it was enough to confirm that the other occupant was indeed Mrs Flemming. There was definitely no way that Janet would be able to fit through the opening as it currently was.

"What's your name love," said Simon to the girl staring up, terror giving way to relief.

"Susan," she answered, her voice hoarse from hours of shouting for help. "You need to help my granny."

"Help will be here soon, Susan," said Simon, hoping someone had been able to find a phone.

"Let's get you out of there and then we can help your granny," said Eugene, reaching for Susan's hands.

She hesitated. "I'm not leaving my granny. She won't wake up."

Eugene looked at Simon with a subtle, but grave expression. "Okay Susan," he said more firmly. "Then we need to get you out to make room for one of us to go in and help her."

Not me, thought Simon.

The young girl finally accepted Eugene's hand. Simon stooped and took her other hand, and together they slowly eased her through the small opening. There was no way that either Simon or Eugene would be able to fit through the tight opening, much to Simon's shameful relief.

While the work to open the doors had progressed, other residents had gathered behind them in the hallway and on the stairs. Eugene's wife stepped forward and put an arm around the young girl, leading her away to sit on the stairs.

Simon and Eugene peered down into the gloom of the elevator. In the little light there was, they could see Mrs Flemming slumped against the wall, head lulled to one side.

Simon turned to where the girl was being comforted on the stairs. "Susan, do you know if your granny has a landline phone?"

"Yes," Susan replied shakily.

"Do you have a key for the apartment?"

"Yes."

Eugene's wife rose and gestured to help the young girl to her feet. "I'll come with you and we can call for help."

Simon turned back to Eugene. "I'll be back in a second. I'll get a torch."

When Simon returned with a palm-sized torch, another neighbour was crouched beside Eugene. She was from one of the other buildings. A wave of relief washed over him. He couldn't remember her name, but he knew she was a nurse, and more importantly, she was petite.

Kneeling beside them, Simon shone the torch into the lift.

"I need to get in there," said the nurse.

"Are you sure?" said Simon, his phobia getting the better of him.

"Yes, can you lower me down?"

She sat down and swung her feet over the lip of the small entrance. Simon's heart rate spiked. She rotated onto her front, and Eugene and Simon took her by the arms and reversed the action they'd just performed on Susan.

Simon positioned the light as best he could so that it illuminated Janet. After a brief examination, the nurse turned and looked up; her face spotlighted by Simon's torch. Her expression suggested it was not good news and a slow shake of her head confirmed it.

"She's gone," she said in a low, solemn voice. "She's been dead for a while. Probably a heart attack."

Simon and Eugene exchanged a wordless look of regret and then hefted the nurse back out of the elevator car. As she brushed herself off, Eugene's wife came to the door of Janet's apartment, a hopeful look on her face. "They're on their way, but it might take them a while. They said they've had a lot of calls this morning," she said. The glum expression from her husband and the others in the hallway betrayed the grim reality, and she and the nurse reluctantly entered Janet's apartment to break the news to her granddaughter.

"We can't find anyone with a working phone," said the man from the third floor, now breathless from running up the stairs.

"It's okay, we found one," said Eugene.

"Good, but there's another problem, the gates won't open," said the neighbour. At that, one of the bystanders on the stairs whispered the bad news to him.

"I'll come down and have a look now," said Eugene with a sigh, lifting his toolbox and giving a final apologetic look towards the elevator.

Simon followed Eugene down the stairs, more for fresh air than any thought that he could be of assistance.

CHAPTER 14

The conference room was still half empty at 8.30, despite the morning briefing being delayed. Lisa wasn't surprised by Christine's absence, but she didn't think so many of the others would also be missing.

"Okay, let's get started," said Barry. "Greg, what's the update from the electric company?"

Greg sat forward and cleared his throat. It was clear from his face that he didn't have good news. "I spoke to the Incident Manager this morning. It's not good," he paused. "They're having trouble getting a clear picture of the extent of the damage."

"Did they give an estimate on the repairs?" asked Barry impatiently.

Greg seemed shell-shocked. Earlier that morning, he'd been relaxed, even blasé. Now he was rattled. "They know there's been significant damage across the entire grid, but they don't have a full report yet. They're having trouble getting through to all their repair engineers."

Lisa turned to Martin, who returned a grave, knowing look.

"I need a timeframe Greg," said Barry.

"They don't know," said Greg.

"What *do* they know?"

"Well, at least two of their main transformers are down and need to be replaced."

"Okay, so how long will that take and how much of the network will that restore?" asked Barry.

"Under normal circumstances each one would take a couple of days to replace, but…" he paused again, "even if they were to replace them, they think there's a lot of other damaged components that'll also need to be replaced before any power could be restored. They can't give a time frame."

"What's your best guess, Greg? Are we talking hours or days here?"

"I don't know."

"Guess!" said Barry, "Give me something."

"I'd say days, at least, if they can get the crews in place and get the replacements," said Greg sheepishly. "It could be much longer, even weeks." Greg looked at Martin but couldn't keep eye contact.

Lisa caught Danny's eye. The hypothetical conversation in the kitchen was now a distinct possibility. She could see from his expression that he was thinking the same.

"Did you say weeks?" said Barry, incredulously.

Greg nodded solemnly. "It's possible, but they really don't know yet."

Barry said nothing. He obviously hadn't considered a scenario where the power would be off for more than a day or two, despite Martin's warnings.

"Barry," said Lisa, breaking the silence, "we were having a conversation this morning about the possible implications on food supplies, if the outage did turn out to be prolonged."

Barry stared at her. *He's out of his depth,* she thought.

"Do we need to inform the army and get them to step in?" she said, half turning to Danny.

Barry looked at Danny, still not sure what to say.

"The army hasn't been given any orders yet," said Danny.

"Once the public realise that the power could be off for an extended period there's going to be a panic," said Lisa. "There'll be looting, particularly as people can't get access to money."

"I spoke to them again this morning, after our conversation," said Danny, "about emergency supplies."

"And what'd they say?" asked Barry, hoping for some good news.

"They've limited stores of basic rations, as I thought, but the main issue they have is with manpower. They've less than 2100 active troops."

"Okay. Well, all we can do is let them know what we know," said Barry. "That it's possible that the outage could be a number of days."

"Weeks," said Martin.

Barry glared at him. "We don't know that. Greg is just guessing."

"So what do we tell the public?" said Lisa. "We need to put out an update."

"I don't know. I need to get through to London again and get direction from them."

"If the army's gonna be setting up food distribution points at some stage, we need to announce that. That might stop people from looting," said Lisa, again mostly directing the statement to Danny.

"I'll update them on the possible extent of the outage and ask them about food distribution," said Danny. "It might take me a couple of hours to get any clear answers from them."

###

Simon stepped out into the bright morning sunlight and noticed a handful of drivers crowded around the keypad for the gate, their cars queued to get out.

As he approached, he could see the look of defeat on their faces. No amount of prodding at the dead keypad, or repeated pressing of their key fobs, would persuade the gates to open.

The group parted as they saw Eugene approach with his toolbox. Their grumblings hushed when Simon told them of the tragedy five floors above. A chorus of sympathetic remarks followed as their various inconveniences were put into perspective.

"Ah, that's awful. I knew Janet, she was a very good barrister in her day," said a woman in a pin-striped business suit.

"Oh my God," said another, praying hands pressed to her lips.

"Fire and Rescue are on their way," said Eugene, setting his toolbox down and taking a knee in front of the control box. "We need to get these gates open to let them in."

The group thinned, some returning to their cars, others moving back to give Eugene space to work.

"What do you think?" asked Simon, looking over Eugene's shoulder into the control box.

"I'm not sure," said Eugene without looking round. "I might be able to get the pedestrian gate open, but the vehicle gate might be another story."

"Anything I can do?"

"See if anybody has a set of jump leads in their car and get one of them to pull up close enough that it'll reach from their battery."

Simon conferred with the waiting motorists, and after a bit of manoeuvring of the cars, handed Eugene the red and black crocodile clips of the jump leads.

Eugene connected a smaller set of wires to those running from the car battery.

"Here goes," he said, with less confidence than Simon would've hoped.

He attached the two clips to wires that he'd exposed in the control box, and with a familiar, piercing buzz, the pedestrian gate beside him clicked open.

"Ha," exclaimed Eugene, seemingly surprising himself.

Simon wedged the gate open with a rock, and Eugene disconnected the power to stop the buzzing.

"What about the other gate?" said the businesswoman.

"I'm not sure," said Eugene. "The hydraulic arms might be a problem."

"I need to get out. I'm already late for a meeting," she said, all sympathy for Mrs Flemming gone. "You need to get them open."

Simon and Eugene glared at her. "Are you serious?" said Eugene. He wasn't one for holding back what he thought. "If it opens, it opens, if it doesn't, it's not my fuckin' problem." He looked up at Simon and rolled his eyes.

Eugene worked at the second control box and, after a couple of minutes, murmured to himself, "Right, let's give this a go."

He connected the cable from the battery and the gate started to hum but didn't budge.

"Simon, give me a hand and we'll try to pull them open now that there's power going to them," said Eugene.

They took a side each and heaved on the large double gates. They didn't move, the hydraulic arms were locked in place. As they stood back, assessing their options, they heard the rhythmic, see-sawing whine of an approaching fire appliance.

The large red appliance pulled up outside the gates and the occupants piled out, fully decked out in their heavy fire fighting gear. Simon met them at the pedestrian gate and filled them in on the morning's events and on their sad discovery. Three of the firefighters headed off into the apartment block, while two others conferenced with Eugene at the main gate.

The ambulance arrived soon after. The paramedics joined Simon, who was talking with the lead firefighter in the carpark. He relayed the information again and without comment, the two paramedics hurried off to the scene.

The woman in the pin-striped suit hovered behind the firefighter. "Excuse me, officer," she said, with an air of authority. "Will you be able to get these gates open soon?" The firefighter looked at her briefly and then back to Simon.

"I'm late for a very important meeting," she added.

"Madam, please stand back while we assess the situation," he said in a professional but firm tone.

"Look, I do a lot of legal work for the fire department and need you to get the gates open," she said, not backing down.

"Madam, with all due respect," said the firefighter. Simon loved that term. He knew it usually meant the complete opposite. "I don't care who you are or who you work for," the firefighter went on. "If we need the main gate open to do our job, then we'll open it, otherwise you'll have to talk to your management company. Now if you'll excuse me." He nodded to Simon and headed into the building to review the situation.

The businesswoman stood speechless, obviously used to getting her own way. She looked at Simon, opened her mouth to say something, then huffed and walked away. Simon allowed himself a secret smile before joining Eugene by the gate.

The two firefighters had decided that the gate did need to be opened, and so had gone to get the necessary equipment from their truck.

"They're gonna disconnect the hydraulic arms," said Eugene. "The battery should then allow it to be unlocked like the small gate."

"That'll keep some people happy," said Simon, tilting his head in the direction of the businesswoman.

"I saw her talking to the fire chief. She didn't seem happy."

"No," said Simon with a wry smile. "He basically told her to piss off."

Eugene looked at his phone again. "I don't understand why none of us have a phone signal."

"This's much worse than a normal power cut Eugene," said Simon. "Apparently it's a widespread blackout caused by a solar storm. Might even be global?"

"Global?" said Eugene sceptically.

"Yeah, a friend of mine's a physics professor. He warned me about it yesterday," said Simon. "He was called in to advise the government. I was speaking to him last night, and he said they were about to put out a public warning, but the power must've gone off before they were able to."

"Right?"

"He says the power could be off for a long time."

"That's not good, especially in these apartments. The gas and the water are pumped by electric pumps in the basement."

"That'll explain why my gas didn't work this morning," said Simon.

"It better be back on by this evening. Liverpool are playing," said Eugene.

They walked slowly back towards the apartment building, neither of them in a great hurry to get back to the fifth floor. The firemen and paramedics would have the situation in hand and there wasn't much Simon or Eugene could do at this stage. Although for Simon it was more the fact that he didn't want to watch them getting poor Janet out of the lift. He didn't exactly know how they'd do it, but he was sure it wouldn't be very dignified.

"Do they know how long it's gonna be off?" asked Eugene as they passed by one of the queued cars.

A waiting motorist, standing by his open driver's door, overheard the question. "They're saying on the radio that it could be days, or maybe even weeks."

Simon and Eugene approached as the man got back into his car and put the passenger window down for them to hear the news report.

"Days? No, that can't be right. I know some of the guys that work on the repair teams for the electric company, they'll be called in and will work round the clock," said Eugene. "I can't see it taking days."

They leaned in close to hear the report. It was a local station giving, what seemed to be, a prepared statement from the government. They then played a clip from an expert.

"That's Martin," exclaimed Simon. "That's the friend I was telling you about, the professor."

In the interview, Martin summarised the information he'd given Simon the night before. Simon thought he came across well, despite the nerves that were clear in his voice for anyone used to hearing him speak normally. His companion was obviously from the government. She gave the typical polished statement, which used a lot of words but said very little.

"You might not get to watch the match after all," said Simon, after they listened to the report.

"We'll see, you never know."

CHAPTER 15

Martin sat quietly in the passenger seat and admired the clean and tidy interior of Lisa's car. He guessed it was a couple of years old, but it looked and smelt brand new, which was probably helped by the *New Car Scent* magic tree hanging from the rear-view mirror. *My car wasn't even as clean as this when I bought it*, he thought.

The ten-minute drive to the radio station had already taken nearly an hour. The rush hour traffic had eased, but every junction was a bottleneck of cars carefully edging out around one another. The dead traffic lights now meant that the right-of-way belonged to the boldest driver.

Evidence of earlier duels littered the side of the road at most junctions. Abandoned cars, with varying degrees of scarring and damage, had been manoeuvred or pushed to the side. One particular crossroads was now manned by a traffic cop who directed traffic around the wreckage of a three-car pile-up, which still blocked most of the junction.

The only vehicles moving at any speed were the emergency services — fire trucks, ambulances and police cars — even they had to slow and pick their way through the chaotic mess at each crossroads.

They passed four petrol stations, each one closed, their forecourts dull and neon signs, which normally showed diesel and petrol prices, now blank. Two had sandwich-boards blocking the entrance with messages written in chunky black marker, blaming the power cut for their closure.

A large supermarket, which would normally have a healthy number of cars in the car park on a Monday at lunchtime, was also closed; the green roller shutters locked in place and another notice taped to the outside. As they crawled past, Martin observed the occasional motorist pull up at the doors. The driver or passenger would get out to read the notice, display animated disappointment, and then return to their car and drive off.

Aside from the occasional comment on the car crashes, Martin and Lisa made the journey in silence, each deep in their own thoughts.

An ambulance squeezing past, siren screaming, prompted Lisa, "Jesus, he's gonna take my mirror off!" She edged her car slightly to the left, alloy wheel now scraping against the curb, in an attempt to give the paramedic another few inches of clearance and hopefully keep her pride and joy intact.

"Things are going to get very bad, very quickly," said Martin as they watched the ambulance weave through the traffic ahead of them.

"Yeah, I think you're right."

"What do you think people are going to do when they hear that the power will be off for a long time?" asked Martin.

"I don't know, but remember we're only authorised to say it'll be off for at least a couple of days," she said, reinforcing the instruction that they'd been given. "We can't even suggest anything else at this stage."

"Humm," replied Martin, still not sure he was comfortable lying to the public. "If I'm asked directly, I'm not going to lie."

"You wouldn't be lying, Martin," said Lisa. "We really don't know yet how long the repairs are gonna take. We'll give another update once we know."

"We both know it's going to be more than a few days," he said, turning to face her. "You heard what your utilities guy said."

"Greg."

"Yeah, Greg. He said himself it could be weeks. I think even that's optimistic."

"Martin, if we tell people that now, there'll be anarchy, people will panic."

Martin looked at her and said nothing. She was probably right. She seemed practical and level-headed and she was the first person to actually listen to what he was saying, even after he told her about the Hale-Bopp thing. He liked her. He trusted her.

"Besides, Danny says the army won't be able to do anything until at least Wednesday," said Lisa.

"I think that might be too late to stop people from taking matters into their own hands."

"Not if they still think the power will be on in a couple of days," said Lisa. "At least by then there'll be something in place to help them."

"I suppose," said Martin.

Lisa returned her focus to navigating the next junction.

"What was the fucking point of that, dickhead!" she screamed, gesticulating to a driver who'd just edged his way forward and blocked her path through the crossroads. "You can't even go anywhere now, you prick." A very unladylike hand gesture followed, which left Martin a little embarrassed, and left the other driver in no doubt as to what Lisa thought of him. Martin stared at the side of Lisa's face, wide eyed and with a hint of a smile.

"What?" said Lisa, an embarrassed smile breaking through her rage. "He could've let me through. He can't go anywhere, anyway."

"I didn't say anything."

Lisa laughed, "sorry that was a bit rude, but it's stressful driving through this."

They finally got through the junction, and the traffic thinned.

"Actually, do you mind if we make a quick detour for a second?" said Martin urgently.

"Where to?"

"It's just this next left. It'll only take a second."

Any further questioning and they'd have missed the turn, so Lisa followed Martin's direction and turned left.

"Just pull up to that gate," said Martin, pointing to the large iron gates of Simon's apartment complex. "I just want to check-in with my friend Simon. I was supposed to meet him last night and I want to let him know what's happening."

Martin got out of the car and approached the pedestrian gate, which was propped open. He wasn't sure how he'd get up to Simon's apartment if the main door was closed. The intercom obviously wouldn't be working. Thankfully, he didn't need to face that problem as he spotted Simon standing with a small group by the door.

Simon saw Martin at the gate, excused himself from the group, and jogged over to meet him.

"Hey, government man," said Simon with a smile.

"Hi Simon, sorry I couldn't get round last night, they needed me to stay," said Martin, nodding towards Lisa, who was waiting in the car.

"They've started listening to you, then?"

"Yeah, well, some of them anyway," said Martin. "That's Lisa. I'm helping her do some radio interviews."

Lisa, having seen Martin gesture towards her, buzzed her window down as he and Simon approached.

"Lisa, this is Simon. Simon, Lisa," said Martin.

"Hey, how's it going?" said Simon.

"Hi Simon," Lisa got out of the car and extended a hand to Simon. "Nice to meet you," she said with a warm smile.

Martin noticed that the handshake lingered a little longer than normal. "Lisa's part of the government committee I was telling you about. She's in charge of getting the public announcements out."

"I wouldn't say I'm in charge. I just put the wording together."

"It's a pity the announcements didn't come out yesterday. You guys should've listened to Martin," said Simon, with a little bite.

Lisa nodded slowly, accepting the slight rebuke.

"Well, in fairness, Lisa was trying to get her boss to do something sooner," said Martin, coming to his new friend's defence.

"We had a nightmare here this morning," said Simon glumly. He leaned back against the front wing of Lisa's car and folded his arms. From the look on Lisa's face, she was not impressed, but she said nothing.

"Did you ever meet my neighbour, Janet?" said Simon.

"Don't think so," said Martin, frowning.

"She got stuck in the lift last night when the power went off," said Simon, sharing his gaze equally between Martin and Lisa. "Her and her teenage granddaughter."

"Shit, that's terrible, must've been awful," said Lisa.

"Yeah, I heard the girl banging this morning about eight o'clock and we were able to get the doors open."

"They were in there all night?" said Lisa.

"Jesus, that would've been about ten hours. Did you get them out okay?" asked Martin.

"We got the granddaughter out, but..." Simon paused, "Janet was already dead. She must've had a heart attack or something during the night."

"Oh my God, that poor girl," said Lisa, covering her mouth with her hands.

"That's awful," said Martin. "Are you okay?"

"Yeah, the Fire and Rescue guys aren't long away. There was only a small gap," said Simon, holding his hands about a foot apart to demonstrate. "Me and another guy were able to get the girl out, but it took the firefighters a couple of hours to get Janet out."

The three stood in silence for a moment.

"I thought I heard something in the middle of the night too," said Simon pensively, "but I didn't check it out."

"Ah now, don't be starting to blame yourself. It's just one of those things. There's nothing you could've done," said Martin.

Simon nodded slowly, but didn't look convinced.

"So what's your plan?" said Simon. "Are you still helping out?"

"Yeah, we're going now to do a couple of interviews with the radio stations."

"Yeah, I heard you this morning," said Simon with a smile.

"That was from last night, but we don't have any better news today, I'm afraid," said Martin. He felt Lisa's eyes burning into him, reminding him that he was not to divulge the true extent of the problem.

"It's okay," he said, meeting her stare. "Simon knows my thoughts on the matter. He knows this isn't a short-term thing."

"So it's as bad as you thought?" said Simon.

Martin nodded, "Looks like it."

"Look Simon," said Lisa, "the government's still trying to work out how long the power's gonna be off and what measures to put in place, so it's important that we manage that information so as not to cause a panic."

"Right," said Simon, raising an eyebrow.

"I'm sure you understand," she said.

"Are you still planning to go to Fermanagh?" Simon asked, turning to Martin.

"Yes, but it might be another couple of days if that's okay?" said Martin. "Were you able to get stuff last night to keep you going for a while?"

"Yeah, that should be fine. Although, I stupidly put my car in the garage last night and put the roller shutter down without thinking."

"Are your supplies in it?"

"No, I brought them all into the apartment."

"That's okay then. We can take my car."

"Okay, sounds good," said Simon. "When do you think you'll be ready to go?"

Martin looked to Lisa, who shrugged, "Not sure, but I'll come and get you."

"We managed to find a way to open the gates, but we'll have to lock them at night, so just beep your horn when you get here. I'll leave the balcony door open so I can hear you," said Simon, nodding up towards his balcony five floors above.

"We should really get going, Martin," said Lisa.

"Well, it was nice to meet you, Lisa," said Simon. "Pity it isn't under better circumstances."

"Yes, you too, Simon."

Simon and Martin walked back towards the open gate as Lisa got into her car.

"She seems alright," said Simon, when Lisa was out of earshot.

"Yeah, she is," said Martin. "Definitely more open-minded than the rest of them."

"Okay, I'll see you when I see you then."

"Yeah, I'd guess Wednesday or Thursday. Take care."

CHAPTER 16

Derek was grateful that they'd an open fire, particularly now, but he hated having to get coal for the damn thing. They rarely lit it, instead relying on the gas central heating, so a large bag of coal from the local petrol station usually lasted a month or so.

He grasped the corner of the bag which was propped behind the door in the small utility room, and lifted it slightly, just enough to check the weight and estimate how much was left. He guessed it'd last the rest of the day and probably the next. He made a mental note to get a bag of blocks or peat briquettes, to make it a bit easier for Jenny when he was back at work the next day.

Holding the small coal shovel, he carefully stacked large bits of coal on top. There was no point trying to put the shovel though the opening he'd torn in the top of the bag, it would fit in okay, but it would come out with only two or three bits of coal and his hand and wrist would be covered in coal dust. Instead, his tried-and-tested method was to put his hand into a plastic bag, of which he had about 300 stuffed into a drawer in the utility room, and then reach into the coal bag and lift out handfuls of coal. He'd then stack as many as he could on the shovel. The same way as he always tried to do one trip from the car with the groceries, he wanted to make do with one trip for coal.

He gently placed the last piece on top of his Ferrero Rocher-like pyramid and focused his stare on it to ensure every piece stayed in its place. He was usually pretty good at negotiating his way back through the house to the living room with the stacked shovel, but today he didn't even get out of the utility room before the pyramid shifted and two bits of coal slid out from the bottom and tumbled to the clean, linoleum-covered, floor. They bounced and skidded across the small room, leaving a black, dusty footprint with each bounce.

"For fuck's sake," spat Derek. He hesitated for a second, considering his options, then pulled the utility room door closed behind him, leaving the mess for his next trip.

"What was that?" asked Jenny, who was gently rocking back and forth on the new feeding chair as she nursed their son.

"I dropped a bit of coal," said Derek. "I'll get it later."

He placed the shovel gently on the hearth beside the fire and used the tongs from the companion set to add a couple of lumps to the glowing fire.

"Is there much left?" asked Jenny.

"Yeah, there's enough for a couple of days," said Derek, "but I'll go and get some logs or peat briquettes, just in case the power's still off tomorrow."

"Do you really think it'll still be off?"

"I doubt it. That'd be three days."

"Can you get more nappies too, when you're at the shop?" said Jenny. "And I think we're nearly out of milk too."

"Okay, I'll check what else we need before I go."

Derek placed the tongs back in their holder beside the fire. Three half used candles sat on saucers on the mantelpiece from the night before. They were the last three they had, so he added candles to his mental shopping list.

He moved to the window and peered out through the vertical blinds, which were tilted open to let in as much light as possible. It was a bright day, so the room was illuminated well enough.

"There was some racket out there last night," said Jenny, as she gently patted the baby's back. The loud belch that followed made them both laugh.

"He sounds like Barney from the Simpsons," said Derek.

Jenny smiled and readjusted the baby to see if he was still hungry. "Sounded like joyriders."

"What time was that?"

"Must've been about 2am."

"I didn't hear anything," said Derek.

"I'm not surprised. You were dead to the world and snoring like a horse."

"I don't snore," Derek protested weakly. "And I've never heard a horse snore, either."

Jenny pursed her lips and raised her eyebrows. "There were a lot of one's shouting too. Sounded like it was a couple of streets away."

Derek glanced up and down the street. It was quiet. He'd seen only one car pass by.

He adjusted the solar charger mat that he'd unfolded on the windowsill and which was slowly charging his phone. He lifted the phone and checked the charge and the signal. Forty percent, but still no signal.

"I'm gonna go out to the car and see if the news is saying when the electric will be back on," said Derek.

Jenny nodded and continued to sway back and forth.

Derek unlocked the heavy front door and squinted as he stepped out from the gloomy hall into the bright, mid-morning sun. As soon as his eyes had adjusted, they fell upon the gruesome murder scene at his feet. Body parts were scattered all around and what was obviously the murder weapon lay beside them.

"Fuckers," hissed Derek, as he looked up and down the street in vain, knowing that the attack was most likely carried out under the cover of darkness, with the perpetrators long gone.

He flicked the fist-sized rock to the side with his foot and bent down to lift Alan's shattered head. Bob had come off even worse. The only recognisable piece of him that remained was his pickaxe. Now Jill stood alone, stony faced, gazing out across the garden. He wasn't a huge fan of the gnomes, but Jenny loved them. He shook his head in dismay. *She's gonna be seriously pissed off that someone used them as target practice,* he thought.

As Derek unlocked his car and looked out at the eerily quiet street, the only life he saw were two figures in hi-vis vests who were talking with one of his neighbours a few doors down.

He turned the radio on. The first couple of stations he tried were playing music, but it didn't take long to find a station with a news report. What he heard was worrying. He was expecting to hear that power was gradually being restored across the country and an estimate for when everything would be back to normal. That didn't seem to be the case. Instead, power was still out across the entire country and would be for some time. Snippets of a recorded interview with a government representative and a local scientist were played;

"I'm joined by government representative Lisa Keenan and Physics Professor Martin Monroe. Can you tell us when we can expect power to be restored?" said the interviewer.

Lisa Keenan? I wonder if that's Ray's sister, thought Derek.

"We are coordinating with the utility companies to get an estimate for the repairs to the power grid, but we do not have a clear timescale as of yet," said Lisa.

Donegal accent, it definitely is Lisa, thought Derek.

"Do you know if it is likely to be hours or days?" asked the interviewer.

"That isn't clear yet, but we hope to have more information later today."

"Do we know the extent of the power outage?"

"It is a national outage, so all areas of the country are affected."

"Some sources are suggesting that this is a global power cut. Can you confirm that?"

"Obviously, with the issues that we are having with communications, we have not been able to confirm the full extent of the situation; however, we do know that all of the UK and Ireland are affected and are still without power."

"Professor, do we know what could have caused such a massive power cut?"

"Yes, it was caused by an electromagnetic storm in the upper atmosphere as a result of a solar flare and coronal mass ejection."

"And in your opinion, is it possible that the power outage could be global?"

"Ah... yes, the data collected before the outage would indicate that a global outage is a possibility."

"Will there be any long-term effects of this electromagnetic storm, other than the damage to the power grid?"

"Well, the damage to electrical components will probably be the only physical damage but as I'm sure you can appreciate, the longer the power's off and communications are down, then the more pronounced the damage to the economy and to society will be..." said the Professor.

"Yes, well, the government are working hard to help the utility companies get the power back on and to minimise the effects of the outage on the public and the economy," said Lisa, seemingly trying to paint a more diplomatic picture than the professor.

Derek found himself pulling an Obama-like sturgeon-face. He was impressed by how professional and grown-up little Lisa was coming across. Ray would mention her every now and again, but Derek hadn't seen her in a few years. He'd always just thought of her as Ray's wee sister, which was unfair but pretty common for a friend's younger siblings, especially when there was a bit of an age gap. They'd see her at the weekend at her dad's birthday, assuming this was all sorted and the big party was still on.

"We're getting reports that people are having issues getting essentials, like food and medicine. Shops and pharmacies are only able to accept cash, that's the few that are open at all, and with the banks closed and bank machines not working, people are finding it difficult to come up with enough cash for what they need," said the interviewer. "Are the government working on plans to address this? Maybe by getting the banks open in some form or helping with food and medicine supply?"

Derek frowned at the question. He hadn't considered that some shops would be closed. He hadn't really thought about the fact that their electricity would be off too, and that their tills and lights and power for their fridges would be off. He just assumed they'd have generators or something. He also hadn't thought that the banks would be closed or that the ATMs wouldn't be working. He really didn't use cash much anymore, except when he was going out to the bar, which he hadn't done in a while. *There might be twenty quid or so in my bedside drawer*, he thought.

He wanted to listen to the rest of the report, but felt a greater urgency to get to the shop and see what the situation was. He was due back in work the next day and had to make sure Jenny had everything she needed, especially if the power was still gonna be off, which, from what he was hearing, was highly likely.

Removing the key from the ignition, he stepped out of the car. As he closed the car door, a voice from close behind caused him to jump.

Derek spun around, a jolt of adrenaline spiking his heart rate. He was very careful and extremely mindful of strangers, particularly when he was getting into or out of his car at his home. He felt especially vulnerable now, in his loose-fitting house slippers, and far from his personal protection weapon, which would normally be strapped to his ankle.

"Mornin", said the gruff but friendly voice. He felt his momentary rush of anxiety fade as he saw the two men in their hi-vis vests. It helped that he'd already seen them further down the street talking to other neighbours.

"How's it going?" replied Derek. His car beeped as he clicked the remote to lock it. The two men approached slowly and stopped a few feet away.

They were in their late thirties or early forties and were dressed in black jeans and trainers. The one who'd spoken was small and heavy-set, like an old-style rugby prop, and wore a long-sleeve sweatshirt. His friend was much taller, with a shaved head and less-friendly, cold eyes. His tight T-shirt revealed huge gym-worked arms and a seemingly random patchwork of tattoos, some professionally inked, others obviously done by an amateur. Both sported lightweight hi-vis vests, which gave them a semblance of officialdom.

"We're from the local resident's group," said the smaller guy.

"I didn't know we had a resident's group," said Derek.

"We're focused mainly from Windsor Drive down to Lee Street, but we thought we'd better spread out a wee bit further to let people know we're available should anybody need help."

Derek nodded acceptingly, but said nothing.

"There's been a bit of unrest and anti-social behaviour over the last couple of nights, since the power's been off," continued the volunteer. "We're mostly checking in with the elderly to make sure they're alright."

The bigger guy remained quiet and just stared at Derek with a slight smile, bordering on a smirk.

"Yeah, my wife said she heard cars being raked last night and a lot of shouting," said Derek, holding the stare of the big guy for a moment before switching to his smaller friend again.

The larger man placed his hand on the roof of Derek's car. It was an awkward stance whose purpose, Derek thought, was less for rest and more to ensure that Derek had a good view of the artwork on the big guy's arm. If that *was* the intention, then it worked. Derek recognised a couple of the tattoos straightaway. He was used to seeing them on a daily basis in work in Bush House, which housed the loyalist paramilitary prisoners.

"Yes, there were a couple of incidents last night," said the first guy. "The police are stretched, so we're gonna have people out on the streets the night to make sure there isn't a repeat."

"Some kids smashed my wife's gnomes too," said Derek, gesturing to the pile of broken gnome-bits by the front door, "but that's hardly the end of the world."

The big guy looked over at the shattered gnomes and broke his silence. "Some people will take any excuse to target a house."

His voice was so high-pitched that it should've been comical coming from such a big man, but instead his icy stare and now definite smirk, sent a chill through Derek. He was starting to feel very uneasy about the encounter with these two visitors. *I'm being paranoid*, he thought.

"Kids, eh?" said the smaller man, with a shrug.

"Yeah," said Derek.

"Anyway, just wanted to let you know that we'll be out and about this evening. Hopefully, the power'll be back on soon and things will get back to normal."

The smaller guy nodded and the two of them started out of the drive to continue their door to door.

"Stay safe now, Derek," said the big guy, with a smile and a nod.

Derek started to reply, but the words stuck in his throat when he heard his name, and he just stood motionless, a tightness building in his chest. *How did that fucker know my name*? he thought.

He watched as they walked further up the street until they disappeared behind a hedge.

"Fuck," Derek said quietly. He stepped over the broken gnomes and glanced up and down the street before locking the door securely behind him. He stood for a moment, contemplating whether to put his ankle holster on. He decided against it. He didn't want to alarm Jenny. She was anxious enough as it was with him going back to work the next day.

Jenny appeared at the living room door. "What's wrong?"

"Nothing," said Derek, faking a smile.

"Who was that?"

"A local community group. They're checking on the elderly in the area."

"That's nice."

"Yeah," said Derek, trying to hide the apprehension in his voice.

"What's wrong?" asked Jenny again, sensing his unease.

"Some wee bastards broke two of your gnomes," he said.

"What?" Jenny spat. "Wee shits."

"I'll make a cup of tea, and then go get what we need in the shop," said Derek, changing the subject. "Although we might've trouble finding one that's open, apparently."

"Why?"

"It was on the radio that most shops are closed and any that are open can only take cash."

"Yeah, I suppose. There's cash up in the bedside drawer," said Jenny.

"Ray's sister was on the news."

"Lisa?"

"Yeah, she was being interviewed about the power cut."

"Did they say when it'll be back on?"

Derek shook his head. "They don't know. They think it might be off for another while. Maybe even days."

"Days?" said Jenny, the worry clear on her face. "We can't go for days. We've hardly any food left."

"I know. I'll find a shop."

"And we need stuff for the baby, nappies and more wipes and Sudocrem - and you're back at work in the morning."

"I know," said Derek. "I'll try to get all that today."

He went through to the kitchen to fill the kettle. His mind was racing. He'd never been a worrier, but he could feel his anxiety building. Thoughts kept coming to him, like persistent waves lapping on a beach, every one posing a question that he didn't have the answer to; why had those guys come to his door? How'd they know his name? Did they know who he was? What he was? Was the attack on the gnomes a warning? Was something happening at the prison? How long could the prison keep running on just a generator? Was he gonna be able to find a shop that was open?

The kettle was overflowing when he finally tore himself from the questions. *Focus on what you can influence*, he told himself.

He'd see if Owens' was open, and if not, try one of the bigger supermarkets.

CHAPTER 17

Simon stood on his balcony sipping his camp-stove-brewed coffee and looked out over his small view of the world.

There were a lot fewer cars on the road today, and those who had ventured out were being considerably more cautious when they traversed the junctions. He'd witnessed one collision the day before, from his crow's nest viewpoint. It wasn't dramatic or spectacular, thankfully. The two cars were travelling slowly, but neither wanted to give way. It was like watching a slow-motion version of *chicken,* where both players won, or lost in this case.

There was drama across the street, however. A group of youths, including the dance troop from Sunday night, were at the front doors of

Heroine Heights. They did not look like a happy bunch.

One sat with his back to the wall, legs drawn up to his chest. He rested his forehead on his knees and hugged his shins tightly. Two others slumped against an old, beat-up Ford Fiesta which was parked on the footpath near the door. It'd seen better days. The sun-faded red paint had almost totally peeled from the dented roof.

Besides them, Fat Head and some new fella that Simon hadn't seen before conducted an animated stop-start argument. He'd no audio from this distance, but the two appeared agitated and aggressive. They'd get in close and unleash a flurry of abuse, then stumble away a couple of steps, possibly to compose another verse of their argument, then return for another angry exchange, their faces getting closer and closer each time. A headbutt, whether deliberate or accidental, was sure to follow.

Simon heard a knock on his apartment door. He looked over the balcony to the gates below; they were both closed, so he knew it must be one of the other residents.

"Hey Eugene," said Simon, when he opened the door to the only neighbour that he really knew to talk to, apart from poor Janet.

"Hi Simon, I'm heading to the shop for a few things, just wanted to see if you needed anything or fancied a trip yourself?"

"I don't really need anything at the minute, but I wouldn't mind getting out for a while. I'll come with you. Where're you going?"

"Just local, I was thinking Owens'," said Eugene.

"Give me a second and I'll get my shoes."

"Sure, I'll meet you down at the gate. I'll get it hooked up."

"Okay."

By the time Simon had made it down to the gate, Eugene had the battery hooked up and the pedestrian gate open.

"We're gonna have to leave this propped open," said Eugene.

"As long as we close it at night, it should be okay," said Simon.

"Yeah, I think I'll bring the battery into the hall at night," said Eugene. "I'll put a notice up to say I'll be bringing it in at 10pm."

They crossed the road and passed by the group of youths that Simon had been watching from above. They looked in a bad state. It reminded Simon of the hangover he'd had the morning after his stag do. He wouldn't wish that feeling on anyone. Only one youth lifted his heavy head to watch the two men go by. His raw eyes tracked them slowly, envious of their pain-free existence.

The road was very quiet, with few cars or pedestrians to be seen. They passed the train station, which was closed. The trains didn't run on electricity, like in some cities, but the signalling system did, not to mention the ticketing systems and the station buildings themselves.

"So, have your toilets stopped refilling?" asked Eugene.

"Yeah, yours too?"

"Yeah, the tank in the attic must've emptied, so the cisterns aren't refilling now."

"I'm having to manually fill the cistern each time," said Simon.

"With what?"

"A mop bucket."

"No, I mean, where are you getting the water?"

"Oh, I filled the bath with water on Sunday before the electricity went out."

"Ha. Good idea," said Eugene, impressed. "I'm gonna have to get water from the river to do that if this goes on much longer."

When they arrived at Owens' the shutters were up and the door open. Simon was half expecting it to be closed, too. There were a handful of customers coming or going. One of them was Derek who he'd spoken to on Sunday. Simon and Eugene reached the door at the same time as the big regular.

Simon smiled and nodded a greeting. "Hey, how's it going?"

"Not bad, thanks," said Derek, tilting his head and raising his eyebrows. "Would be better with electric though."

"Yeah, I know, it's nuts."

"I don't ever remember a power cut lasting this long before."

Simon and Eugene both shook their heads in agreement.

As the three entered the shop, Simon saw that the lights were off, and the coolers and freezers weren't chilling.

Seamus mustn't have been able to get a generator, he thought.

Instead, the shop was dimly lit by a handful of battery-operated camping lanterns, which supplemented the meagre light coming through the narrow window above the door.

The front door was wedged open and a handwritten sign said, "Cash Only. No credit given!".

"You have cash, okay?" Simon asked Eugene.

"Yeah, I've a few quid, you?"

"Yeah, I got some from the bank machine on Sunday, just in case."

"Shit, you were well prepared. Thanks for the heads up," laughed Eugene.

Another sign taped to the chest freezer just inside the door read, "Free meat. If you can cook it, please help yourself."

Apart from themselves and Derek, who was now seeking out various items and filling a basket, there were only two other shoppers in the store. Simon approached the counter, where Seamus sat on his usual perch.

"Hey Seamus," said Simon. "You weren't able to get your hands on a generator, then?"

"No, I couldn't get through to the hire company. I've been trying them since yesterday morning."

"I didn't expect you to be open at all."

"Well, I figured people will still need groceries and I have to try to get rid of all the stuff that was in the fridges," said Seamus with a sigh. "There's still some sausages and maybe even a couple of steaks in the freezer down there, if you have some way to cook them."

"Yeah, I have a wee camp stove."

"Well, help yourself to whatever you want, no charge. I'll have to throw them out at the end of the day, anyway."

"That's great. I'll have a look, thanks."

"If you're needing anything else though, I'm only able to take cash, I'm afraid. The till and the card machine are down."

"That's okay, don't think I need much, but I've some cash anyway if I do."

Simon stepped aside to let another customer set his basket on the counter and went to check out the fridge. There was still a decent selection of meats that'd either been frozen or had been in the chiller until the power cut. He lifted out a packet of sausages and two shrink-wrapped rump steaks. The steaks were starting to darken a little at the edges, but as long as he cooked them today, he thought they'd be fine.

A raised voice caught his attention. The customer he'd left at the counter had now been joined by another, and they were in a heated discussion with Seamus.

"There's nothing I can do about it," said Seamus. "The card machine's down so I can only take cash. I put a sign on the door."

"Well, the bank machines aren't working, so this is all I've got," said the man bluntly.

"Well, I'm sorry, but I can't help you."

"Why don't you take a note of what I owe you, and I'll sort it out when the electric's back on?"

"Yeah, I'll do that too," said the second customer, a forceful statement rather than a question.

"Look, if it was just you, then I could do something like that. But if I do it for you, then I'd have to do it for everyone and I've already refused people credit today as it is, so I'm sorry I can't do it."

"No one else needs to know," said the first guy.

Seamus slid down off his stool and stood at the counter. "I'm sorry, no. There's some meat in the fridge down there that I'm happy for you to take, but I can't give credit."

Simon looked around. Eugene was at the far end of the shop and didn't seem to have heard the argument yet, although the volume was beginning to rise. Derek, however, had heard the exchange, and although not solely focused on it, Simon could see that he was keeping one eye on the proceedings and edging his way towards the till as he continued his shopping.

Simon didn't really want to get involved. He could see both sides of the argument and if he was honest, he wasn't really one for confrontation.

"Well look," said the shopper, packing some items into the bag-for-life that he'd brought with him, "I am taking these things and I'll drop the money in to you as soon as the power's back on."

"No, you're not," said Seamus, putting his hand on the bag that the man was filling.

"I'm sorry mate, but I'll have to do the same," said the second man.

"You can take what you can pay for, or you can get the fuck out," shouted Seamus, as he tugged on the canvas bag. He wasn't gonna let anyone take advantage of him or steal from him.

Maybe I should say something, thought Simon. He didn't like that both customers were putting pressure on the elderly shopkeeper.

"I'm sorry, but this is an emergency and you're not gonna stop me," said the customer. "I've told you I'll bring you the money when I can get it. Now let go of the bag."

Simon had to do something. He took a step towards the counter and was about to speak when Derek beat him to it.

"Guys, you heard the man," said Derek in a firm, authoritative tone. "He can't give you credit."

Both customers turned and looked at Derek, who seemed even taller than normal. He'd moved to within three feet of the counter.

Derek glanced at Simon, who was a step or two further back on the other side of the two men. "We're not gonna let you leave here with stuff you haven't paid for."

The two men noticed Simon's presence when Derek purposely glanced towards him.

"We need to feed our families," said the second man, a little less confidently.

"The power's only been off for two days. You're hardly gonna starve. Make do with the basics," Derek nodded to the bag that the first man was filling. "A six-pack of Cadbury Cream Eggs is hardly survival food."

The angry customer looked down sheepishly and slowly lifted the chocolate eggs out of the bag.

Eugene appeared alongside Simon, aware that there was tension. "Everything alright?"

The two men looked around again and seemed to accept that they weren't going to be allowed to leave with more than they could pay for. They re-prioritised their items and left with a fraction of what they'd hoped, glaring defiantly at Derek and Simon as they made their way to the door.

"Thank you lads," said Seamus when the two disappointed shoppers had left. "I'm glad you were here."

"Are you here on your own for the rest of the day, Seamus?" asked Simon. He was concerned, and Seamus looked a bit rattled.

"Yeah, the wee girl hasn't made it in today."

"I think you should close up for the day," said Derek. "There's probably gonna be more arseholes like that."

Seamus huffed and thudded his wooden club down on the counter. "I can handle anyone who thinks they can steal from me."

Derek made eye contact with Simon and raised an eyebrow. "I'm sure you can, Seamus, but then you'd be the one in the shit. It's not worth it."

"Yeah, but what about decent people, like yourselves, who need things?"

"We can go to the bigger shops for a day or two for anything we need," said Simon.

"Yeah, well, maybe you're right," said Seamus, reluctantly agreeing.

Derek placed his own basket on the counter, and Seamus started toting up the bill on a large calculator. Simon waited patiently for Eugene to finish his shopping.

The battery-operated radio behind the counter chirped with the familiar opening jingle of a news report and the newscaster gave the headlines, which hadn't changed much since the report Simon had heard that morning.

After the summary, they announced another interview with experts from the government; it was Martin and Lisa again. Simon, strangely, was as happy to hear her voice as he was to hear his friend Martin's. He'd been thinking about Lisa since they'd met the day before and felt a pang of guilt for that.

Eugene joined the group at the till as they listened to the latest interview. There didn't seem to be any good news and certainly no update on the likely timescale for restoring the power. They did mention that the army would be setting up food distribution points in all main cities and towns in the coming days if the power wasn't restored.

"Is that your mate again?" Eugene asked Simon.

Derek frowned at Simon and tilted his head slightly. "The professor guy? Do you know him?"

"Yes, he's a good friend of mine," said Simon. "He warned me the power cut was coming on Sunday."

"That's funny, the girl, Lisa, is a friend of mine, well my mate's wee sister, actually."

"Seriously? Ha, it's a small world," said Simon. "I met her last night. Her and Martin, the professor, called at mine."

"Yeah?"

"I'm supposed to be going with him to his family holiday home in Fermanagh until this's all over," said Simon, "but he's been held up helping the government."

"Ha, really is a small world," Derek said with a smile.

Simon and Eugene headed back towards their apartment block. Derek had offered to stay with Seamus until he locked up, although Seamus insisted on serving a couple more customers who came as they were leaving.

Simon had picked up a few more items, and some more bottled water, along with his free steaks and sausages. Eugene had taken

Simon's advice, stocked up on more than expected, and even had to borrow some cash from Simon to get everything he thought he'd need.

The two men walked back across the railway bridge with two heavy shopping bags each, Simon offering to carry one of Eugene's. They talked about the confrontation in the shop and how easily someone could find themselves in that position.

"I don't agree with what the guys were doing," said Simon, "ganging up on an elderly man, but I could see how you could find yourself in that position very easily."

"Yeah, shit, if I hadn't been able to get this stuff, we'd have been pushed for anything to feed the kids," said Eugene. "Certainly by tomorrow anyway, things would've been pretty desperate."

"From those guys' point of view, they weren't stealing. They were gonna give him the money when they were able to get it from the bank," said Simon. "If you put yourself in their shoes, they probably thought that was a perfectly reasonable proposal."

"Yeah, but if Seamus was getting that same line from every customer who didn't have cash, then you could see how he had to say no."

"Absolutely. It's a tough situation."

"But if we hadn't been there, and that other guy especially," said Eugene, "things could've got out of hand."

"Yeah, I don't think Seamus would've let them go without a fight."

"Did you see that fucking cudgel?" laughed Eugene.

Simon smiled. "I don't even know if he'd need it. I'd say he's a hard enough wee man for his age."

"Could've been a nasty enough situation."

As they crested the top of the hill, passing the passengerless train station, they saw the group of suffering youths again. Some stood like wet cloths hung from a hook, and the poor soul, who'd been hugging his knees, was now curled in a foetal position, gently rocking. Fat Head and his sparring partner had called a halt to their verbal jousting and now studied their feet as they paced slow circles in front of the doorway of their apartment building.

When Simon and Eugene got to within ten yards, the nearest youth lifted his huge head and locked on to them.

"Here we go," said Eugene. "Just keep walking. Don't engage with them."

"Yeah," said Simon.

The youth shuffled towards the footpath so that he'd be within a couple of feet when the two men got level with him, "Alright mate," said Fat Head. "Have ye got a feg?"

His blood-red eyes were framed by wide, panda-like circles, and with his pallid skin, he would've made the perfect extra in a George Romero zombie movie.

Eugene ignored him and walked on.

Simon was too polite to ignore anyone. "No, sorry fella, don't smoke."

The youth looked at the bags of groceries. "Where'd you get the stuff? Is Owens' open?"

Simon angled his body slightly towards him but kept pace with Eugene. "Yeah, but he's closed now until the power comes back on."

The other youth, who was still on his feet, ambled over to join Fat Head and the two followed Simon and Eugene as they crossed the road towards their gate.

"What about you mate," the youth called to Eugene. "Got a feg you can lend me?"

Eugene turned when he reached the gate, which was still propped open. "No, don't smoke," he said coldly.

"Have ye any food you give us, mate," said the second youth, now a little too close to Simon. "We're starvin' mate."

"No, sorry."

"You've two full bags," spat Fat Head. "What about some water?"

There was definite menace to his tone, but Simon also heard the desperate plea of someone just trying to get through a terrible illness. He felt sorry for them.

Eugene stood at the gate and stared at Simon, willing him to ignore the drug addicts and get through the gate so that he could close it.

"The food isn't mine," said Simon, pausing at the gate, "but here take this." He handed over one of the two litre bottles of water, as he did so he was enveloped in a bubble of stale human and cannabis-aired clothing. Simon swore he could taste it rather than smell it. He hurried to join Eugene.

Eugene kicked the rock to the side and clicked the heavy metal gate closed.

"You shouldn't have give them anything, fucking junkies," said Eugene, as they entered their building.

"Looked like they needed it," said Simon, glancing back.

The two youths stayed by the locked gate as they passed the water between them, drinking greedily. Simon knew it was the right thing to do.

CHAPTER 18

Derek woke to the buzzing of the alarm on his phone. That's really all his phone had been useful for over the last three days. It was 6.30am, still no signal.

"Morning," whispered Jenny, who lay beside him with their son tucked in beside her.

"Morning. Sorry, did I wake you?"

"No, I'd just finished feeding him. Hopefully, he'll sleep for a few hours now."

Jenny had been getting up to do all the feeds since the power had gone off. There was no way to store or warm the expressed milk now, so Derek was of no use at feeding time, although he did usually get up to provide moral support.

Jenny had been careful not to wake him this morning, though, as she knew he'd an early start.

"The electric's still off?" asked Jenny.

"Yeah, there's still no phone signal, either."

"How long's this gonna last?" she whispered. "What'd we do if it goes on for days?"

Derek didn't know how to answer. He just shook his head slowly.

"I'll light a fire for you before I go so that the place's warm when you get up."

Jenny gave a tired smile. "Thank you."

He leaned over and kissed her on the forehead. "I'll see you tonight."

"Be careful."

Derek couldn't bear the thought of another cold shower, so he had a pits n' bits wash at the sink and used a generous amount of deodorant. He'd have a shower in work, he told himself.

He lit the fire as promised, ensuring that it was stacked with enough coal to keep it going for at least a couple of hours, and got dressed in his uniform for the first time in two weeks.

He decided to put his shoulder holster on today instead of the more discrete ankle holster he normally wore. He was still a little spooked from the day before, although he'd more or less convinced himself that he was being paranoid.

He opened the gun safe in the hall and slid one of the magazines into his personal protection weapon, racking the slide to put a round in the chamber. It was against his safe handling training, but he didn't care. A fraction of a second could be the difference between life and death. He strapped it into the holster and adjusted his overcoat to make sure it was concealed.

Before approaching his car, Derek checked up and down the street. It was early, so the street was quiet. He rounded the car to the driver's side and, with another quick glance around, he dropped into a press-up position. He scanned the underside of the car. Nothing seemed out of place or foreign. He'd started to become a little complacent about his safety routine lately, especially the checking of his car.

Every petrol station on Derek's route was closed, and the metal shutters were down on all the shops, even those that would normally open at 7am. The roads were deserted, and he passed only a handful of pedestrians in total.

Derek slowed when he saw blue flashing lights ahead. Two police cars were parked beside a small supermarket. It didn't have a roller shutter and the large window beside the front door was smashed, with glass and debris strewn all around. A small group of police officers stood with what was likely the owner. It was clear that the shop had been looted during the night. Desperation had obviously set in for some people who'd probably been unable to access cash for supplies.

Derek was lucky that he'd been able to find enough cash and that Seamus Owens' had been open the day before. But even still, he'd only got enough essentials to last another couple of days, and their cash was almost gone.

What's it gonna be like by the end of the week? It was a worrying thought. They better get the bloody power on soon.

The motorway was similarly quiet, and apart from a few abandoned cars on the hard shoulder, probably out of fuel, he saw less than a dozen vehicles along the ten-mile stretch of road, four of those had been a small convoy of army vehicles heading towards the city. *At least they're mobilising*, he thought.

He pulled up to the gates of the prison and was waved through the barrier by gate security.

After checking his firearm into the armoury, he went through to the office to find Ray.

Ray Keenan was also a Senior Prison Officer and shift leader, and with Derek out on paternity for the last two weeks, he'd been doing extra hours to cover staff shortages. He was now just coming off a sixteen-hour shift. His last task was to do the handover to the incoming Senior, Derek.

"Am I glad to see you," Ray said, as Derek entered the office and placed his backpack on the chair.

"You look like shit," said Derek.

"I haven't left here in three days, but it's your shit-show now, big man," said Ray, with a half-smile, half-grimace.

Derek frowned when he saw the seriousness on his friend's face. "How bad is it?"

"Bad!" Ray replied, all humour having gone from his voice.

"Where's the Governor?"

"He was here on Monday," said Ray, "not that he was of any use. He just sat in his office all day."

"What about yesterday?"

"Yeah, he was here for a couple of hours. He said he was trying to get through to the army but couldn't get them on the phone, so he was gonna drive to the base in Antrim. He never came back."

"Were you able to raise the brass?"

"The landlines are still working, but every time we try headquarters we get an engaged tone. We've been trying for two days, so I think their switchboard's down. We did get through to Magilligan. They haven't heard anything either."

Derek scratched his head and planted himself across from his drained and defeated looking friend, "I assumed there would've been orders, or some kind of direction".

"Magilligan are in the same boat as us, running on generators, low on food, water and staff," finished Ray.

"Okay," said Derek, sitting forward and trying to muster some leadership skills. "What's our status?"

"The generator's powering the lights, CCTV and the boilers for the heating, but we're running very low on fuel for it. I'd say we'd be lucky to get through tomorrow," said Ray. He seemed glad to get started on the official handover.

"We haven't had a delivery since Friday, so we're out of fresh food and, other than soup, we're down to two days of emergency rations."

Derek sat back in his chair. He hadn't fully considered how bad things could get in the prison if the power and communications didn't come back on. *What the hell were they supposed to do by the end of the week if it hadn't?* he thought.

"But that's not our worst problem," Ray said, spinning a notebook round for Derek. "We had two suicides last night."

"Jesus!" Derek studied the incident report. "Johnston and O'Kane? They weren't on the watch list, were they?"

"No, Johnston had only been here a few weeks, but with how little staff we have, it wouldn't have made a difference, anyway. We haven't enough bodies to cover even the ones on the list. They're climbing the walls in there and with the rumours and the little bits of news flying around, it's like a pressure cooker ready to blow."

"How many were you missing on the last shift?" asked Derek, thinking of his crew, who should be starting to arrive. *Hopefully.*

"Four. One from B-shift stayed on, but the others were leaving whether I let them or not," said Ray. "It'll be interesting to see how many turn up for you."

"Yeah, I wouldn't be surprised if we had a couple of no shows. It's getting a bit crazy out there," said Derek. "A lot of car wrecks 'cause the traffic lights are out and arseholes out rakin' about in stolen cars. The police are supposedly very stretched so there're groups of youths hanging around, and I saw one shop on the way in that'd been looted. You can really feel the tension."

"Looted? Seriously?"

"Looked like it."

"Shit, that's nuts. The power's only been off for three days," said Ray.

"Yeah, but most of the shops are closed and the ones that are open are only accepting cash, which most people don't have a lot of," said Derek. "People get desperate pretty quickly when they can't feed their families."

"Yeah, I suppose so," said Ray. "Sorry mate, I didn't even ask about Jenny and the baby. How're they doing? I saw your photos on Facebook. He has Jenny's looks, thank fuck."

"Ha, very funny. Yeah, they're fine, he's sleeping well thankfully. Jenny's freaking out, though."

"I'm sure she is."

"I heard your Lisa on the radio yesterday. Sounded very professional."

"Yeah, I've heard a few interviews the last couple of days," said Ray. "She phoned me on Sunday night to warn me about the power cut."

"Yeah? They knew about it in advance?"

"It was only a couple of hours before it happened."

"Thanks for the heads-up, buddy," said Derek sarcastically.

"I thought it was only gonna be off for a few hours. I'd no idea it was gonna be like this," said Ray defensively. "I don't think Lisa really did, either."

Derek pulled his chair in and took out his own notebook. "Right, shift change is in thirty minutes. Take me through the details."

The two friends walked to the staff room in silence. Derek had never experienced such a dire situation. He wasn't voicing the true extent of his anxiety and he guessed Ray was the same.

The briefing room was about the size of a school classroom. It had six desks with chairs evenly spaced in two rows, although most people stood around the edge of the room, during the briefings, with their backs to the large whiteboard, or various notice boards and charts along the walls. It was here where staff members reported at the start of their shift.

A door on one side led out to the staff car park past the changing rooms and armoury.

The armoury secured all the prison's firearms, riot gear and equipment, as well as serving as the temporary store for officers' Personal Protection Weapons, while they were within the prison. A door on the opposite side of the briefing room led to the prison proper.

The room had started to fill with the early shift staff. Twenty-eight officers and support staff were expected, but when Derek and Ray entered, they were shocked to find that only sixteen had reported for the shift. Fourteen officers and two civilian staff. None of them were happy to be there. They milled around in small groups, swapping whatever news or gossip they had from the previous two days since the start of the blackout. The common thread was the anger and disbelief at the apparent lack of action from the government.

Derek and Ray exchanged a grim look, "This isn't enough," Ray whispered. Both men were still standing away from the main group. "I'd twenty-four last night, and we barely kept the place in check. This isn't safe for anyone, Derek."

"I know, but what the fuck do we do?" said Derek quietly, before moving to the front of the room.

"Okay, everyone. Let's get started," said Derek, raising his voice to get the room's attention.

"Is this it? Is this all we've got?" said one of the officers.

"Where's the Governor?" someone else asked from the back of the room.

"It seems so, unless we get some latecomers. Some people might be delayed," said Derek.

"Derek, this isn't enough to cover the shift," said Thomas, an officer who'd been in the service nearly as long as Derek but, for one reason or another, hadn't moved up the ranks as Derek had.

"Okay, look, I'm not gonna bullshit you. This is not a good situation," said Derek, raising his hands to fend off any other questions or comments. "Let me update you on what we know and we can take it from there."

There were grumblings from the group, but no one else interrupted.

"This power cut is going on longer than any of us expected and with the communications issues, we haven't been able to get through to head office. The Governor has also been trying to get through to the MoD to ask for assistance. He wasn't able to do so yesterday, so he left to try to get speaking to someone in person. We don't have an update on that yet."

Derek moved closer to the group and leaned against one of the desks in the front row. "I'll not lie to you. We're in pretty bad shape. We're running on generator power, as you know, and the fuel situation for that isn't good. The food situation is bad too. We urgently need a delivery."

"Boss, it isn't safe to try to run this place with this many staff," said Thomas.

"I know Thomas, we're working on finding a solution," said Derek.

Ray stepped up beside Derek. "I'll be staying, and I'm gonna get some volunteers from my shift to cover, too."

Derek glanced at him and raised an eyebrow. He knew Ray was running on empty and had been pulling double shifts to help cover Derek's paternity leave, but he was grateful for any help he could get.

"I'll be focusing this morning on getting the assistance and the supplies we need," said Derek. "We'll maintain full lock down while we're running on reduced staff."

"What if the power doesn't come back on before the generator runs out?" asked one of the civilian staff. "I heard on the radio that this could last for days or even weeks."

"Hopefully it won't come to that. They're working on getting the power back on, but we'll review the situation throughout the day and I'll keep you all informed."

"Something needs to change soon, boss," said Thomas.

Derek nodded. "Yeah, it does. Okay, your team leads will give you a revised list of duties."

As the room began to empty, Derek and Ray made their way back through to the office. He'd never experienced anything like this before. He'd had staff shortages before, but he'd always been able to call for help and he couldn't think of a time when the army had been used to supplement prison staff.

Ray slumped onto the worn-leather three-seater couch in the office. "So what's the plan?"

Derek didn't answer straight away. There were so many problems to solve, it would've been easy to let them overwhelm him. He took his seat and placed his elbows on the desk, resting his chin on his clasped hands. His day had only started, but his face was already etched with the pressure and stress of the situation.

"What do you think are the chances of the Governor having any joy with the army?" said Derek.

"I'd say if he was coming back with any help, he'd have done so by now."

"Okay, let's run through the options," said Derek.

"I think we have to assume the worst, that the electric isn't coming on anytime soon," sighed Ray. He looked exhausted.

"Okay, let's assume it doesn't. The army's our only option then."

Ray nodded slowly. "That, or we open the doors and let them all out."

"Let the prisoners out? Are you serious?"

"What alternative have we?"

Derek sat back and folded his arms across his chest. He still wasn't sure if his friend was joking or not. "Where would they go? It would take sixty trips in the minibus and what do we do just drive them all into Belfast and drop them off? Do we just let them walk out the gate and find their own way home? Some of these guys are murderers and rapists. What do you think would happen when they reached one of the houses down the road? Faced with a twenty-mile or more walk, what do you think they'd do to get their hands on one of the cars from those houses?"

"We could maybe let some non-violent ODCs out and some that are on remand," said Ray.

Derek ran his hands through his hair and interlaced his fingers behind his head, "But we'd still have the problem of what to do with them when we let them out. We'd be putting the local community at too high a risk."

Ray stood and began to pace the small office. "So what then? Do we just lock the doors and walk away? Let them all starve?"

"I don't fucking know, Ray," Derek snapped.

Ray stared out the window, looking at nothing but searching for inspiration. The room fell silent.

Derek realised that he'd been a bit sharp with his friend, who had every right to clock out and leave him to sort this mess on his own, "I wish my son had have held on for a week or so," he said with a wry smile.

"Oh yeah, so you'd still be on leave and I'd be left with this shit."

Derek leaned forward again and ran his hands slowly down his face, resetting his composure. "Right. So, as I see it our only solution is to bring in the army, agreed?"

"Agreed, but how do we get them?"

"Right. First thing we have to do is send someone to the nearest army base to explain the situation and request support."

"Jesus, we've little enough people here as it is," said Ray.

"I know, but you said you were gonna see if some of your crew could stay on," said Derek, hatching what he thought might be a decent plan. "Ask as many as you can, but for those who say that can't stay, ask them to call into the army base closest to where they live on their way home. And get them to phone us with an update when they make contact, assuming they can."

"Okay, that might work."

"But we really do need at least four or five of them to stay if we're gonna get through the day," said Derek gravely. "Otherwise we'll have a mutiny on our hands."

"A lot of them have already been covering for others and have been on long shifts," said Ray.

"Okay, tell anyone who can stay, to use the infirmary and to get a couple of hour's sleep, including yourself. You look like you're about to drop."

"Yeah, okay, as long as we've everyone on duty by lunchtime, not that there's much food to give the inmates."

"In the meantime, I'm gonna continue trying to get through to anyone who can help and I'll check the state of the generator fuel."

"Oh, Trevor Baker and also Ciaran O'Hare are demanding a face to face with management," said Ray. "I told them you'd speak to them when you got in."

"Oh great, thanks."

Baker and O'Hare were the spokesmen for Bush House and Roe House, the two paramilitary wings of the prison. Each wing had its own little leadership committee, made up of the most senior members from each of the many flavours of paramilitary organisations on each side of the divide, but Trevor Baker and Ciaran O'Hare were recognised as the lead spokesperson on each side.

The loyalist and republican wings were separated by the other wings that housed the Ordinary Decent Criminals. Derek always thought it strange, referring to a criminal as *decent,* particularly when some of them were far from it; like child-molesters, murderers and rapists.

"Okay, I'll go and see them this morning," said Derek.

"I wouldn't leave it too late, tensions are getting pretty high, particularly in Roe," said Ray.

Ray left to try to persuade some of his team to stay, and to recruit others for the vital mission to the army bases.

CHAPTER 19

Derek gathered his thoughts and then made his way to Bush House to see Trevor Baker, the loyalist spokesperson. If he remembered correctly, it was on Baker's arm that he'd seen the same tattoo as that of the visitor in his driveway the previous day. He'd pushed aside his paranoid thoughts of the two hi-vis clad community workers, but they were starting to surface again.

He walked through the deserted main hall, which would normally be full of inmates playing cards or drafts at the small tables or taking turns on the pool table. Today, all inmates were confined to their cells, except at mealtimes.

Derek had been working in prisons for nearly twenty years, and he still hadn't got used to the distinctive odour; a mixture of body odour, stale feet and toilet waft.

He'd worked out once that there was an average of one dump being taken in the prison every minute of the day. Nine hundred prisoners, assuming an average of one bowel movement per inmate per day, over a sixteen-hour waking day, equated to fifty-six dumps an hour or just under one per minute. *The things you think about as a prison guard*, he thought.

As he passed the row of cells, some prisoners shouted questions, "Boss, any word on when the electric's comin' back on?" said one.

"This isn't fuckin' right. Why do we have to be stuck in our cells?" shouted another.

Inmates appeared at the barred doors of the cells as he walked by. He ignored most questions, but as he passed the last cell, the prisoner, a disgraced doctor who'd been given twenty years for euthanizing six elderly patients, beckoned him over.

"Mr Henderson," the doctor said in a quiet and respectful tone. Derek had known the former doctor for over ten years, since he'd first been convicted. They got on well.

"Hi Brian," said Derek, taking a couple of steps closer to the doctor's cell.

"Is there any update on when this power cut is going to end?"

"They don't know yet Brian, they're apparently working on it, but they haven't given a timescale yet," said Derek with an apologetic shake of his head.

"Things are getting pretty bad in here Derek," said Brian. "Everyone's anxious about what's going on out there and there's rumours that we're running out of food."

"I know Brian, trust me, we're working hard to sort it out. It shouldn't be too much longer," said Derek.

There was a mutual respect between the two men, even though they were on opposite sides of the bars, and Derek had never felt the need to lie to him before. He could hardly tell him the true extent of the crisis, or the fact that they were running out of options. Derek could see from the doctor's eyes that his poker face had failed him.

He turned and took a few steps towards the middle of the hall. "Okay everyone," he raised his voice to try to reach all the cells. "I know you all have questions and are pissed off about being on lockdown."

"Fuckin' right we are. This is against our human rights," shouted one prisoner.

"The power's still off and because of that, we've some staff shortages. That's why we've had to put the temporary lock down in place. I know it's not good and we're trying to find a solution," continued Derek.

"What about the food?" shouted another inmate.

"We're expecting a delivery soon," said Derek. It wasn't exactly a lie, but he wasn't confident that any of their regular deliveries would be coming anytime soon. He hoped the army would be able to sort that issue too. He turned and continued through the hall, nodding sheepishly at the doctor.

Derek took a seat in one of the small interview rooms and waited for the guard to escort Baker in.

Trevor Baker entered the room and took a seat opposite Derek at the small grey table. He was a tall, lean guy in his early fifties. The jet-black hair that he'd come into the prison with had gradually greyed over the eight or so years that he'd been Her Majesty's guest. He folded his wiry arms across his broad chest and sat back in his chair. With his plain light-blue shirt sleeves rolled up, Derek could see the tattoos that Baker wore with pride. He'd been right. He recognised the same patchwork of symbols on Baker's forearm as he'd seen the day before.

"Well Trevor, you wanted to see me?" said Derek.

"I've been asking to see the Governor since Monday," said Baker sharply. "This lock down isn't right."

"The Governor's away trying to find a solution to our staffing problems so that we can relax the lockdown."

"When will he be back? We need answers."

"Answers to what?"

"Don't take me for a fool, Mr Henderson," Baker leaned forward, voice calm and low. "We know what the situation is. The power isn't likely to come on anytime soon. The generator's bound to be running low on diesel and from the shite that you're serving us in the kitchen, there hasn't been a delivery in a while."

He sat back again and smiled. The smile causing a small scar on his left cheek to crease noticeably, which was why he'd acquired the nickname of *Bum Cheek*, not that many people would call him it to his face.

"So, what answers do you want?"

"We demand to know what you're doing about it. When will we get proper food? When will we be allowed out of our fuckin' cells?" his calm demeanour was starting to fade. "You can't keep us locked in cages like fuckin' animals." His volume increased, and he unfolded his arms.

Then, as suddenly has his temper had flared, it was gone, and he sat back in his chair, the flick of a mental switch had restored the facade of control, "What happens when the generator runs out of fuel?" he said, with a calm, near gentle tone.

Derek held the prisoner's stare. Convincing the other inmates that everything was under control, and that there was nothing to worry about, was one thing, but the guys in Bush House, and even more so in Roe House, were a different prospect. They were always probing for information, testing, playing minds games. With every conversation, they were trying to find a weakness or gain an advantage. If ever he needed a poker face, it was now.

"Trevor," Derek said calmly, raising his eyebrows to emphasise. "Yes, we have problems with the power, and with some supplies to the kitchen, but we're working hard to resolve them and if the power isn't restored soon, we've procedures in place to deal with that scenario."

"What procedures?" said Baker, the heat in his voice rising again, as though his temper was controlled by a faulty thermostat. "We've a right to know what's going on. We're stuck in here with no way to contact our families." Then, perhaps more unnervingly, his calm quickly returned. "We've no way of knowing how our families are coping with this blackout," he said in a quiet and congenial tone. "I'm sure you understand that, Derek..."

"It's Mr Henderson or Sir," corrected Derek.

"I'm sure you understand that, Mr Henderson. You have a family yourself now, don't you?"

Derek held his breath and stared at the inmate. He could feel his own temperature rising, but he didn't react.

"It's a difficult situation for everyone," said Derek, forcing himself to keep a professional tone. "We'll update all the inmates as soon as we've more information."

"That's not good enough. I want to know what you plan to do if the power doesn't come back on soon. You're gonna have to release us if things get worse," said Baker, leaning forward again. "You can't keep us locked in here under these circumstances."

"Guard," called Derek to the officer waiting in the hall as he rose from the table.

"We're not finished here, Derek," said Baker, spitting Derek's name.

"Yes, we are," said Derek as the officer entered the room to escort the prisoner back to his cell.

"We've a right to know that our families are safe," Baker raised his voice as the officer took his arm and started to guide him towards the door. "Is your family safe, Derek? In your nice wee house with your three fuckin' gnomes…"

"What the fuck did you say?" Derek yelled, his professional deportment shattered in an instant as he rounded the table in two quick strides. Without another word, he grabbed the prisoner by the throat and drove him through the open door into the corridor, brushing the startled officer aside.

He pinned the man to the wall on the opposite side of the narrow hallway, his right arm strained as he lifted the surprised inmate onto his toes. The two men locked eyes. All that Derek needed to say was said with a deadly stare. Baker's eyes began to water from the constricting grip, and Derek's from his primal rage.

The smaller prison officer forced his way between the two men, breaking Derek's grip. He glared at his boss before bustling the gasping prisoner down the hall towards his cell.

In normal times, such a reaction would result in a formal complaint and an investigation, and likely serious repercussions for Derek, but these weren't normal times, and he didn't care either way. All he could think about was his family. The broken gnomes, the two hi-vis community workers who knew his name. *The fucking tattoo*, he thought. He needed to get home to his family.

Derek paced back and forth in his office. He had a hundred things he needed to do, but the multitude of thoughts bombarding him left him unable to focus on any of them. He was sweating; he was breathing heavily, and the anxiety clenched like a fist in his chest.

The office door opened and a tired but smiling Ray entered. "Good news. I managed to persuade four staff to stay for another shift. Two of them need to go home first for a couple of hours, but they'll be back before lunch."

"That's great, thanks."

"Jesus, what's wrong with you?" said Ray, noticing how agitated his friend was. "You okay?"

"I just had a run-in with that prick Baker," said Derek sternly.

"What do you mean, a run-in?"

"He threatened my family."

"What? What the fuck did he say? What did you do, Derek?" asked Ray, afraid that his friend had done something he'd regret.

"He asked if my family was safe, but it was the way he said it," said Derek, realising that it didn't sound that much like a threat.

"What do you mean?"

"He started saying about Jenny's gnomes in the garden. Someone smashed them the other night and then those two guys from his crew came to the door yesterday."

"Whoa, slow down. What are you talking about? What guys?"

"Two guys were going around the doors yesterday. They said they were from the local residents' group and were checking on the elderly in the area."

"So, why'd they come to your door?"

"They didn't. They came up to me in the driveway."

"So what makes you think they were with Baker?"

"Same tattoos."

"And what'd they say?"

"Nothing really, but they knew my name."

"Right. And the gnomes?" asked Ray with a shake of his head and scrunched-up face.

"Jenny has three gnomes in the garden."

"Really? Gnomes?"

"Yeah, I know, they're stupid fucking things, but someone smashed them with a rock."

"And you think it was something to do with Baker?"

"I don't know, but he mentioned them."

"Okay look, it's obvious that they know where you live and if it was the republicans then yes, it'd be a bigger problem, but think about it, there's no way these guys could've been communicating with anyone on the outside since Sunday night. When did you say this happened?"

"Monday night."

"Okay, so it must be a coincidence. He's just trying to wind you up."

"Well, it worked."

"What'd you do?"

"I just pushed him against the wall."

"Did you hit him?"

"No."

Ray raised his eyebrows questioningly.

"No, I didn't hit him."

"You're over-thinking it mate."

"Maybe it's just freaked me out a bit," said Derek, still pacing. "I'm worried about Jenny and the baby."

"Are you able to call her?"

"No, we don't have a landline in the house. I'm on a double shift today, too."

"Okay, look, I'll stay another day. You head on at five and I'll cover this evening for you."

"I can't ask you to do that Ray, you're
heading up to your folks', aren't you? They'll be
expecting you."

"It's okay, I'll go tomorrow."

"Okay, thanks, but let's see what happens
today. Did you get anyone to volunteer to go to
the army bases?"

"Yeah, Teresa Murray lives near the base in
Antrim. She's gonna call in and explain the
situation."

"Okay, thanks Ray. Maybe I'm just
overreacting," said Derek, finally taking a seat
at his desk. "But you need to go and get at
least a few hours' sleep."

"Yeah, I will. I'm running on fumes," said
Ray, heading for the door.

"And Ray, thank you."

CHAPTER 20

Lisa and Martin left the Thursday morning STAC briefing with mixed feelings. Apart from the two of them and Barry, only two other people had turned up. The latest absentee was Danny, who'd been coordinating with the army.

In Wednesday's briefing, the day before, Danny had reported that the army was mobilising to set up relief points in every city and major town. Each of the five cities would have between five and ten relief points, with at least one relief point in each of fifty other main towns across the country. That would mean between 100 and 150 different relief points, each needing to be set up, manned and supplied to provide food and water to nearly two million people. A logistical nightmare. An impossible task, with only two thousand troops, Danny had said.

The army had divided the operation into two strands; one to locate, secure and transport the supplies of food, and the other to distribute them. The supplies would come first from their own stores of emergency ration meals, and when those had run out, from the many warehouses around the country which held supplies for supermarkets and shops.

The legality of such a move was questionable, but thankfully some General or high-ranking officer had made the decisive call to act now and face the consequences later.

Martin agreed straight away with Danny's opinion of the operation, although he didn't see the point in voicing that fact. With about half of the troops dealing with supply chain, only about one thousand soldiers would be available to man the relief points. That would mean less than ten soldiers per site, not enough to provide crowd control, never mind operational security.

With Danny missing, Barry had asked Lisa to go to one of the relief sites and observe. But first they had to deliver a hand-written list of relief point locations to the radio stations. Once that announcement went out on the radio, Lisa expected the relief points to get very busy, very quickly.

Lisa asked Martin to go with her. She didn't specifically need his skills or knowledge, but she sensed that he didn't want to stay behind at the office.

She hadn't intended for Martin to stay for so long; she hadn't even expected to still be here herself. She was supposed to be on annual leave from Wednesday, but with so many people not turning up to the STAC meetings, she felt like she had to stay and help. There really wasn't much more the STAC could do, anyway. They were really only supposed to be giving science and technology-based advice to the decision makers, but at this stage there wasn't much else they could advise on.

Lisa drove *her* car again. Martin had offered to take his, but she couldn't let him do that. He'd been good enough to give up his time. She couldn't ask him to use his fuel too. Although she had considered it when she saw that her's was now down to half a tank. She'd have just enough to make it to her parents' in Donegal.

They called to the two main radio stations in the city and gave an update about the relief points, leaving the list of locations with the stations for them to read out. It wasn't going to be the most exciting listening as the DJ read out a list of over one hundred locations, but if people were desperate enough for assistance then they'd surely endure it as they listened for the location nearest them. Antrim and Armagh residents would certainly be happier than those living in Warrenpoint or Whitehead.

"Right, we should go to the relief point at City Hall," said Lisa. "Hopefully they're set up and ready to go now that the stations will be announcing the locations."

"Yeah, I don't think it'll take long for crowds to start to gather," said Martin.

They drove the short distance into the city centre and parked a couple of streets from City Hall. The streets were quiet. A group of taxi drivers, optimistically waiting for paying customers, huddled by their taxi rank.

As Lisa and Martin approached on foot, they could see the large khaki-green army trucks parked inside the grounds of the landmark building. The side gates of the perimeter fence were closed and locked, so they continued to the front entrance.

The front gates were also closed, but Lisa caught the attention of a soldier who was standing inside, a few yards away.

"Excuse me," she called through the thick, ornate, wrought-iron gates.

The soldier pretended not to hear her at first and when she persisted, he waved her off, "The relief station isn't open yet. Please come back in an hour."

"Excuse me," she shouted again, this time reaching through and waving her government ID in the air. "We're from the government. We need to see your commanding officer."

The soldier approached and studied her identification and then her.

"We've been helping to coordinate these relief points," she said. "We've been sent to observe. We need to speak to your commanding officer."

"Yes ma'am," said the soldier.

He removed a bunch of keys from his belt and unlocked a padlock that was securing a heavy chain to the gate, swinging it open just enough for the two of them to enter. The soldier locked the gate again and beckoned for Lisa and Martin to follow him.

"Sir," said the soldier as he approached an officer who was coordinating the off-loading of one of the trucks. "This lady and gentleman are from the government. They're asking to speak with you."

The officer nodded curtly to the soldier, who took the nod as his order to return to what he was doing. "Captain Dogherty, how can I help you?"

"My name is Lisa Keenan. This is Professor Monroe. We're from the Science and Technology Advisory Cell, we've been asked to come and observe."

The captain reached out and shook hands with each of them; a sharp and efficient handshake. His grip was firm enough that it hinted at his strength and conditioning, but not purposely, so that it would be intimidating. Lisa could see he had sufficient confidence that he didn't need to prove it with a knuckle crunching grip.

"Well, there isn't much to observe yet," said the Captain. "My orders are to set up a relief station here and distribute HDRs to the public."

He moved towards one of the two large transport lorries which were parked side by side on the front lawn of the huge Neo-Baroque building. The trucks' wheels sank into the soft turf under the weight of their loads. The forbidden sweet scent of diesel filled the air.

"Sorry, what are HDRs?" said Martin, beating Lisa to the same question.

"Humanitarian Daily Rations," said the Captain.

From the back of each truck, a soldier was passing boxes to others on the ground, who were then stacking them on pallets beside the main gates.

"What's in them?" asked Lisa, stepping up and looking at the writing on the side of one of the boxes.

"Each pack is designed to cover an average adult's daily calorie requirement," said the Captain. "It's not a gourmet meal, but they're actually not that bad."

Lisa looked at the rows of pallets that'd already been off-loaded and stacked. There must've been about fifty pallets.

"How many do you have for here?" asked Lisa.

"These trucks are doing one more run and after that we'll have one hundred pallets with fifty boxes on each," said the officer. "That's 50,000 HDRs."

"So, each box has ten meals in it?" asked Martin.

"Yes, we're planning to give each person a full box. That should keep the average family going for a couple of days."

"So, are there more deliveries coming tomorrow?" asked Lisa.

"There won't be any more HDRs. All the stock we have is being distributed across the country today," said the officer. "Any future supplies will come from civilian warehouse stocks."

"So what way will that work?" asked Martin. "I mean, these HDRs are nicely packaged, self-contained meals. The stuff from the warehouses is going to be a selection of everything, I assume."

The Captain folded his arms and sighed. "Exactly, that'll be a big problem."

"What do you mean?" asked Lisa with a frown.

"It'll be a manpower problem," said the Captain, moving to a foldout table under a gazebo that was acting as a command point. "We're stretched enough as it is, trying to manage the distribution of these boxes today." He pointed to a roughly sketched layout of the grounds of the City Hall, which showed the different gates with small x's at various points.

"I've only ten personnel here, plus myself. I'm planning to have the public filter through the front gate in two lines, pick up their box and proceed out through the side gates," he pointed to the gates on either side of the building.

"That means if we've one man on each exit gate, two on the entry gate and two plus myself on the inside distributing the boxes, then I only have four left, to patrol the outside and keep order," he looked at Lisa with eyebrows raised as if expecting her to understand his predicament straightaway.

It all seemed well thought out and plausible to her, so she didn't react.

"It's a security and logistical nightmare," he said. "It might look like a good plan on paper, but things never go according to plan. I have no contingency if something goes even slightly wrong, which it will."

Lisa slowly bobbed her head in understanding.

"Now imagine tomorrow, if we're trying to organise the distribution of anything other than these neatly packaged, self-contained boxes of ready meals?" he said, reusing Martin's description and sweeping his arm towards the row of pallets.

"Who makes up the boxes of assorted goods that would need to go to each person?" asked the Captain rhetorically, "Either it's done at the warehouse where they're as stretched as we are, or we'll have to do it here, and that'll be impossible with only ten men."

"I see what you mean," said Lisa, understanding the officer's concerns.

"If we don't keep control of the crowd in a situation like this, then things will turn ugly and dangerous very quickly."

"How can we help?"

"Do you have access to any personnel through your department?"

"No, I'm sorry we don't."

"Most of the committee aren't even turning up anymore," snorted Martin.

Lisa shot him a glare, which she quickly softened as she remembered he was there as a volunteer and she was extremely grateful for his help.

The Captain shrugged, as if expecting that to be the answer. He was just going to get on with it.

"If I could get you a handful of volunteers, would that help?" asked Lisa.

"Yes, anything would help," said the officer, hopefully. "It would let me put more men on security."

"Leave it with me," said Lisa. She nodded for Martin to follow her and headed towards the front gate.

"You think you know where you can get volunteers?" asked Martin. "We don't have much time. I'm sure the announcement will have gone out on the radio by now."

"I know. I'm just gonna ask people on the street to help," she said. Her plan was no more sophisticated than that.

The soldier on the gate let them out, and she told him she'd be back in a few minutes.

With her back to the gate, Lisa looked up and down the street. She started to feel like she'd given the Captain false hope. There was hardly a person in sight.

"So what now?" asked Martin.

"Maybe we just ask the first few people who turn up."

Martin looked around, then back at Lisa and raised an eyebrow.

"Hold on, I'll be back in a minute," said Lisa, and she jogged off across the street towards the taxi rank.

Five minutes later, she returned to the front gate, followed closely by six taxi drivers. She waved the gate soldier over and ushered them inside; the soldier looked like he wanted to protest, but he assumed the Captain was in the loop.

Lisa asked the volunteers to wait as she approached the Captain again, "Six volunteers any use to you, Captain?" she said with a smile.

The Captain looked over at the bunch of volunteers, who contrasted greatly with his own men in terms of physique and attire, but for whom he seemed very grateful. He smiled at Lisa, "Very good Ms Keenan, you don't hang about, do you?"

He turned to one of the soldiers helping to unload the trucks and gave him some instructions while gesturing to the group of volunteers. The soldier ran off.

"One thing though," said Lisa. "I promised them two boxes each at the end of the day for their help."

The Captain stared at her for a second, then nodded. "That seems fair enough."

Lisa re-joined Martin, who was talking to the soldier at the gate. In the few minutes that she'd been talking to the Captain, a crowd had started to grow outside.

"The announcement's been broadcast, it would seem," said Martin.

"Looks like it," said Lisa. "It'll be interesting to see how many turn up."

CHAPTER 21

Derek pulled into the staff car park. He was tired. He'd spent a restless night, reacting to every noise, loaded handgun in his beside drawer, unbeknownst to his wife, of course. He hadn't shared with her the details of his run-in with the loyalist leader, nor his concerns about Tuesday's visitors. She was anxious enough as it was; she didn't need to be worrying about stuff that probably wasn't real.

Before turning off his engine, he noticed that his car had only a quarter tank of fuel. He'd have to fill it from the petrol pump at the prison, which was normally reserved for the prison vehicles. It was completely against the rules, and he was sure it wouldn't be the last rule he'd break that day.

Derek found Ray slumped at his desk when he entered the office. His demeanour confirmed to Derek that he did not have good news.

"Hey," said Derek.

"How's it going? Jenny okay? No trouble last night, I assume?" asked Ray.

"Yeah, she's okay, no trouble," said Derek. "So what's the story? Any luck with the army?"

"No," said Ray flatly.

"Did you not hear from Teresa?"

"I did. She called from the base while she was there and put me on to a lieutenant who was the highest-ranking officer there."

"And what'd they say?"

"He said they can't provide any assistance," said Ray, still stunned by the news that he was relaying. "He said that all personnel, including the Army Reserve, have been deployed to set up humanitarian relief for the public."

"Humanitarian relief? Is that what he said?" said Derek, the anxiety that he'd been fending off since the day before washed through him. "Did you not tell him we have a humanitarian crisis right here?"

"That's exactly what I said."

"What did he say?"

"He said he understood the situation, and that there was absolutely nothing he could do to help," said Ray. "He said the only reason he was still in the base himself was because he was on crutches. He said every last man and woman was engaged in the ongoing relief effort."

"Did you explain to him what options that leaves us with?"

"I did. He said all he could do is report it to his superiors, but that we shouldn't hold out hope of assistance coming anytime soon."

Derek lowered himself onto the couch. "Fuck."

The two men sat in silence for a long moment.

"What are we gonna do, Derek?" said Ray, eventually. His voice was shaky, and there was panic in his eyes.

Derek made brief eye contact, then sat quietly, shaking his head.

Eventually he spoke, in a low and detached voice, "What options do we really have? If we don't have enough staff to safely manage the prison today, then what can we do?"

"Let them out or lock them in," said Ray, staring vacantly at the desk in front of him. The gravity of the statement, and the consequences of either option, prevented him from making eye contact with his closest friend.

"We can't let nine hundred convicted prisoners just walk out the gate," said Derek, affirming the thought to himself rather than responding to Ray. "We're in the middle of the countryside, there's no transport, no communications... we can't do it."

Ray bobbed his head in agreement.

"So, where does that leave us? We just lock the doors and walk away? Leaving nine hundred men to starve to death in their cells?" said Derek. He leaned forward and cradled his head in his hands.

Silence descended again as the two men contemplated the horror of the situation.

"Did the Lieutenant give any indication of when they might be able to send resources?" asked Derek, clutching at straws.

"No, but I think we can assume it won't be for a couple of days at least," said Ray.

"Okay, so if it was only a couple of days, that might not be the end of the world," said Derek, trying to draw some hope from Ray's answer. He couldn't allow himself to think that it was false hope.

"What are you thinking?"

"We leave the paramilitaries in charge."

Ray snorted, then realised his friend was not joking. "You're fucking serious. They'd tear each other apart."

Derek stood and walked to the far end of the office. He studied a layout of the prison that was pinned to a corkboard on the wall. "We can divide the prison into two. Baker and his ones can have control of Bush house and the two adjoining blocks of ODCs, and O'Hare and his crowd can have Roe house and the rest of the prison. Look, if we only give them access to these areas," he pointed to the sections on the layout that he was referring to, "and keep these two corridors locked, then we can keep them apart."

Ray stood beside him and regarded the diagram which he'd never really looked at or even noticed before. He knew the prison like the back of his hand and visualised the areas that Derek was describing.

"Do you think they'd agree?" asked Ray.

"Do they really have any choice?" said Derek, feeling slightly less paralysed now he had a possible plan, no matter how bad a plan it was, "The alternative is that we lock everyone in their cells with no access to food or water."

Ray considered Derek's idea. Problems with the plan kept coming to him, but he could see no better alternative.

"What about the sex offenders? You think they'll be safe?" asked Ray.

Derek chewed his lip. "I don't know. We could make it clear to Baker and O'Hare that there'll be consequences if anyone gets hurt. Tell him that the army will be here at any time."

"There's what, twenty-five in Roe house and sixteen in Bush?" said Ray. "How's each group gonna control over four hundred prisoners?"

"Well, they're organised. They've a form of hierarchy and discipline, and they've a reputation," said Derek, trying to build a justification for the plan that he'd now set his mind on. "Plus, we'll put them in charge of the water and the rest of the food supplies. They can use that to try to keep order."

"Jesus, that might have the opposite effect," said Ray.

"Fuck Ray, I don't have all the answers, but it's the only thing we can do as I see it."

Ray nodded slowly.

Derek looked at his watch. "But you never know we might be surprised and have enough staff to keep going."

Ray sighed, "I can't see it."

"Well, let's go and find out."

The two senior officers stood at the front of the staff room as the clock on the wall ticked to 8.30am. The two men exchanged a knowing look. *Decision made*, thought Derek. Only twelve staff stood in front of them, which was nowhere near enough to run the prison.

"That's it then. We have to abandon the prison," said Derek quietly and without looking at his friend.

"Fuck, when you actually say it out loud..." said Ray. "This is madness."

"I know."

"Boss," said one officer who was in a small huddle with three others, "we've been talking here and we're not prepared to go on duty with just the twelve of us."

"That's right Derek," said another officer, who stood in another small cluster. "You can't expect us to do this. It's not safe."

Others voiced their concerns, and their reluctance, or outright refusal, to start work. Derek stepped forward and raised his hands to quieten the group. "Okay, I hear you. And I agree," he paused. He couldn't believe what he was about to say. "We've been trying since the start of the week to raise our concerns about the staffing and other issues. We haven't been able to get through to head office. We've also officially requested support from the army."

"When do they get here?" asked the first concerned officer, expecting Derek to ask them to hold the fort until the army arrived.

"They're not coming," said Derek.

Murmurs of anger and confusion filled the room.

"So what happens now?" said one officer.

"We've been discussing the options," said Derek, gesturing to Ray beside him. "The only two options we see are to either let all the prisoners out—" the room irrupted again with gasps and snorts.

Derek raised his hand again and continued, "That's obviously not an option." The room quietened again. "The only other option is for us to withdraw."

"What does that mean, withdraw?" said one of the civilian staff.

"We need to work out the details exactly, but we intend to withdraw all staff and lock the prison until the army gets here."

"And what happens to the inmates?"

"We'll leave the prisoners with a limited amount of access to certain areas so that they can access food and water," said Derek.

"You can't be serious," said the same staff member with a laugh. "You're gonna leave the prisoners in charge of the prison?"

"We'll be dividing the prison in two. We'll leave Roe House in control of one side and Bush House to control the other," said Derek in a clear and decisive tone.

The staff member continued to murmur his protests within his small group.

"If any of you have a better solution to this problem, then please shout," said Ray.

No one came forward with a better plan, and the murmuring subsided.

"So, how do we withdraw? What's the procedure?" said a staff member.

"We need a couple of hours to plan it so that we can execute it safely," said Derek. "So we need you all to assist those currently on duty for the next couple of hours, then we'll all leave together."

Derek had the incoming staff replace the night shift and ran through the same announcement with them, fielding similar questions. Again, no one could come up with a better approach. They all agreed to stay for the two hours that Derek said he needed to finalise the details.

Derek still held out a glimmer of hope that the cavalry would come riding to the rescue within those two hours, but he made his plans anyway.

CHAPTER 22

Derek and Ray finalised the plan for how they'd safely retreat from the prison. As they did, they continued to try to get through to head office, the police and the army.

Derek was eventually able to get speaking to a senior police officer. It'd taken over an hour of waiting on hold, but it was progress compared with previous days. He may as well not have bothered. The police were having their own staffing issues, and according to the superintendent, those that were on duty were stretched to breaking point. The only thing he could advise was to request assistance from the army.

Derek had tried again to get through to various army bases and to the MoD offices, but with no joy, the cavalry wasn't coming.

"Okay, so that seems like the most sensible plan in terms of withdrawing staff," said Derek, as they finalised the details.

"Yeah, so we tell Baker and O'Hare at the last minute?" said Ray.

"Yeah, I think that's best, and while I'm doing that, everyone else withdraws to the staff room and we leave from there."

"We'll need a chain and padlock to lock the main gate from the outside," said Ray.

"Do we have one?"

"Yes, there's one in the utility shed out the back."

"That reminds me, I'm nearly out of fuel. Before you leave, can you fill my car from the pump out there, please?"

"What do you mean before I leave?" asked Ray, "We're leaving together, right?"

"No, I need you to leave before we do this."

"What? Why?"

"I'm the senior officer, Ray, and this is my shift. I'm making the decision to withdraw from the prison," said Derek forcefully. "I'm gonna lose my job for this, at the very least. I don't want it falling on you, too."

Ray protested, and the two men argued until it was clear that Derek wasn't gonna have it any other way.

"I need you to do one other thing," said Derek, while Ray sat on the couch, sulking like a teenager. "I need you to load up all the firearms from the armoury and anything that could be used as an offensive weapon and put them into my boot. I'll bring them to a police station."

"Okay will do," said Ray.

"You should do that now, and then head on," said Derek.

Ray motioned to protest again, but he knew there was no point.

"Are you going straight to your folks' place?" asked Derek.

"Yeah, you should get Jenny and the baby and follow me up," said Ray. "You were planning to come up anyway for the weekend, you should get out of the city for a while."

"Yeah, I'll try," said Derek.

Ray reached out for a handshake, which turned into an embrace. "Okay, I'll see you soon," he held his friend at arm's length. "We had no other choice here, Derek."

Derek stared at his friend and sighed. "I know, but it doesn't make it any easier."

"I'll sort your car out and leave your keys on your desk," said Ray. "Get this done, then get Jenny and the baby, and get on the road, right?"

"Okay."

Ray left to carry out the last couple of tasks before leaving. Derek went round his staff and spread the word of the withdrawal plan and timescale. There was no turning back now.

It was time for him to visit O'Hare and Baker. O'Hare was usually the one that he was least keen to sit in front of, but today, given the incident the day before, he was dreading talking to Baker. He wasn't sure if he could hold his temper.

Derek took two officers with him and spoke to O'Hare first. He outlined what was about to happen and what he expected from O'Hare and his crew. After the usual rant on human rights and demands to be freed, given the extreme circumstances, O'Hare soon settled, and in the end seemed to be happy enough with the arrangements.

Next stop was Bush House and Trevor Baker.

Derek walked through the adjoining block, as he'd done the day before, this time trailed by the two officers. As before, he got a barrage of questions and demands from the prisoners; he ignored them all. As he passed the last cell, he saw Brian, the doctor, standing at his cell door.

"Mr Henderson," called Brian.

Derek paused for a beat and looked at him, then put his head down and walked on. *He was likely condemning this man and the rest to death?* he thought.

The guard brought Trevor Baker into the small room as he'd done the day before, but this time, he and the other officer stayed in the room with Derek.

Baker looked at them crowded into the tiny space and smiled. "You don't trust yourself Mr Henderson?" he said, gesturing to the two officers.

"Something like that," said Derek.

"So what's the story? Are you letting us out?"

"No," said Derek. "I'm giving you the keys."

Baker drew up his cheeks and squinted in confusion. "What?"

"We don't have enough staff to safely operate the prison, so I've taken the decision to withdraw until the army assumes control."

"When will that be?"

"Soon," said Derek. "Likely within the next forty-eight hours, but we don't know exactly when."

"And what do you expect us to do?"

As he'd done with O'Hare, Derek explained the expectations, and the consequences should anything happen. He outlined how, if things went smoothly and Baker's men were able to keep control and keep the rest of the inmates safe, there would be very positive benefits for them, and that it would most likely lean heavily in their favour going forward.

Baker saw through Derek's attempt at carrot and stick psychology. He sat back and folded his arms, eyes boring into Derek's. "You're leaving us here to die, you fucking prick."

"There's enough water, and there's food for a couple of days," said Derek. "Believe me, we considered leaving you locked in your cells."

Baker leaned forward and smirked, "I believe in Karma, Mr Henderson, Sir," he said quietly. "People reap what they sow."

Derek resisted the urge to pick up where he'd left off the day before. Instead, he slid a large bunch of keys across the table and nodded to the two officers.

The three men left the room and headed back through the cell block. They didn't run, but they quickened their step to make sure they got back to the safety of the corridor, that neither paramilitary group had keys for. They wanted to make sure they were out before the two new key-holders let their respective followers out of their cells.

The remaining staff gathered in the staff room. The hushed conversations ended when Derek entered.

"I want you all to know that this is solely my decision," said Derek solemnly. "We tried every option. We couldn't get through to head office, and the police and the army were unable to send help."

"There was nothing else you could do, boss," said one of the officers.

"I'm hoping that the army will be able to get here in the next couple of days," Derek continued. "Obviously, there's gonna be an investigation into this when everything's up and running again. I expect you all to cooperate with that investigation and to tell them that I gave the order to withdraw. None of this is on any of you."

The staff filed out, heads hung low. Some approached and spoke to him on their way out. He barely heard their attempts at reassurance or affirmation of his decision.

He retrieved his car keys and the thick chain that Ray had left on his desk, then did a final check to make sure Ray hadn't missed anything in the armoury. The gun safe was empty, as was the ammunition safe. The locker that normally held the PAVA spray canisters and the ASP batons was cleared out, too. All that remained was the rack of protective gear that the Tornado teams used during riot situations. He left them and locked the two heavy doors.

His sense of dread built with every door he locked behind him as he made his way out to the car park. He opened the boot of his car and unzipped the large canvas kit bag that Ray had stowed. Inside were the two Ruger Mini 14 rifles, which those assigned to the guard towers would be issued, two boxes of 5.56 NATO rounds, the pepper spray canisters and six extendable batons, and his own carry case with his Glock 26 and two magazines inside.

He removed his Glock, inserted the magazine, and clipped it into his holster under his left arm. He closed the boot and leaned heavily on the lid. He was nauseous, the tension and dread close to emptying his stomach.

He followed the last of his staff down the short driveway and stopped just beyond the huge gates. He heaved them closed and threaded the chain through the bars. Then snapped the heavy padlock closed with a metallic click. That was it, it was done. *God help me*, he thought.

He taped a handwritten notice to the small reinforced window on the guard hut beside the gate, then got into his car and drove off.

CHAPTER 23

Simon spun the little fold-out arm of his windup radio in an attempt to charge it enough to listen to the latest news. The thing was next to useless. He'd bought it online prior to a camping trip that never actually happened, so it'd sat in the box for years. Ten minutes of frantic winding would give about five minutes' worth of listening time if he was lucky.

Restoration of the power seemed no closer. The army was now being drafted in to distribute supplies at relief points all over the country. An exhaustive list of locations was read out at the end of the news report. Thankfully, Simon's nearest one, at the City Hall in Belfast, was one of the first on the list. He didn't really need emergency rations, but he thought it'd be good to be able to bring something with him to Martin's place. He also needed to get out of the apartment. Cabin fever was setting in as he waited for Martin. The twenty-minute walk would do him good, too.

The streets were surprisingly busier than when he'd last ventured out. It wasn't quite like a normal Thursday afternoon in the city, but there was a reasonable number of people out, all travelling in the same direction as him. Presumably all with the same destination. It would seem that with no time to prepare, and therefore no plans in place, three full days without electricity was about the right time frame for people to start to need state aid.

The closer he got to the centre of the city, the more people he saw. When he crossed intersecting roads, he could see that the streets running parallel to his were the same. Ahead, individuals were converging into groups or even a crowd. In the absence of any notable traffic, a noticeable din of voices was building.

Simon turned his last corner and saw the large, ornate government building two blocks ahead. The source of the rising noise was now evident. As newcomers coalesced, the growing crowd swelled and flowed onto the vehicleless streets. The demand for assistance was much greater than Simon had expected. There must've been thousands, if not tens, of thousands of people swarming around the fenced compound of City Hall.

A small but steady trickle of individuals was emerging from the throng, each carrying a cardboard box as they pushed against the surging tide. They'd answer questions from expectant queuers as they went, each curious as to the contents of the mystery box for which they themselves were waiting.

As Simon got closer, he could see the leading edge of the crowd was being directed by a handful of soldiers. They attempted to corral the surging mass and restore the orderly queueing that was likely in place when the relief station had opened. They were failing. As more people arrived and added to the growing numbers, the soldiers' sphere of influence reduced and they slowly retreated until they controlled only the immediate area outside the front gates.

Simon was still at least fifty yards from the front gate, with a sea of determined aid-needers between him and his own cardboard box. He climbed a small set of steps at the front of a shop front across the road from the relief station. He now had a better vantage point and could see over the fence into the compound. There were army trucks and rows of the cardboard aid-boxes stacked on pallets. Just inside the gates was a table where those lucky enough to get through the gate were collecting their package and moving to the exit.

Simon also had a better view of the mayhem on the outside of the front gate. The soldiers were fighting a losing battle to keep order. Scuffles and arguments were breaking out as people jostled for position and tried to barge their way through or defend their hard-earned ground.

Simon shook his head and made the decision to abandon any hope of getting through and collecting an aid package. It would take hours for him to swim his way to the front and by the looks of it, they'd be dangerous waters. It wasn't worth it. He'd walk back by Seamus' place and if he was open, great, if not, he'd make do with what he had and just wait for Martin, wherever the hell he was.

###

When Derek had appeared home in the middle of the afternoon, Jenny knew straightaway that something was wrong, and his ghostly complexion affirmed it. He broke down when he saw her. The strain of what he'd done, and the fate of the men under his care, was too much to hold in. He explained the events, including the run in with Baker and his fears about the two men in the driveway.

Her concern for him, coupled with his uncharacteristic show of emotion, soon outweighed her anger at being kept in the dark. She agreed they should pack up and get out of the house as soon as possible. He was sure they'd revisit the topic of his lack of honesty soon enough.

Their plan was to go to Ray's parents' place in Donegal. They'd stay there until the power and communications were restored, then he'd come back to face the consequences of his actions. But first he had to get someone to take the firearms that now sat in a kit bag on his kitchen table. He'd have to put his own weapon in storage too, as he wasn't permitted to take it over the border into the Republic of Ireland. Normally, if he was crossing the border or taking a trip abroad, he'd store his weapon in the prison armoury or in a local police station. He'd tried two police stations on his way home. Both were closed.

"What are you gonna do with those?" asked Jenny, when she entered the kitchen and saw Derek standing over the bag of weapons.

"We'll need to surrender them before we leave," said Derek.

"Where? A police station?"

"Yeah probably, but I tried two on the way home and they were both closed."

"Closed?" said Jenny, surprised. "Why were the police stations closed?"

"They were only small stations, but I assume for the same reason that I abandoned a prison full of men."

Jenny said nothing.

"I was gonna bring them to the army relief point in Lisburn, but I couldn't get anywhere near it," he said. "There was just too many people."

"There's one set up at the City Hall. We could try there," said Jenny.

"Yeah, we could try that. If not, then we'll go to one of the bigger stations."

They hurriedly packed the car with everything they'd need for a few days away, which was mostly stuff for the baby, and locked the house. Derek felt uneasy and exposed as he ferried things out to the car, but he didn't see anything that concerned him. Nevertheless, he was relieved when they pulled out of their street and headed towards City Hall.

They got no more than a few hundred yards when Derek braked and pulled in suddenly. He pulled up behind a parked police car and got out of the car.

"What are you doing?" asked Jenny.

"I'm gonna give the bag to these guys."

Derek approached the passenger side of the police car, but before he got there, both doors opened and the two cops got out, seemingly not happy with someone approaching them in their car.

"Can we help you, sir?" said one officer.

Derek approached, but was careful to stay a few feet back so as not to unsettle the on-edge officers. "Yes, please, my name is Derek Henderson. I'm a Senior Prison Officer at Maghaberry prison."

"Okay?" said the driver, rounding the back of his patrol car.

He had his prison identification and firearms license already out of his wallet as he stepped closer, offering both to one of the officers. "Firstly, though, I should tell you that I'm carrying a concealed firearm."

Derek slowly opened the left side of his jacket to reveal his holstered pistol.

The two cops stiffened slightly and exchanged a look, but soon relaxed again when the one examining Derek's ID nodded. "Okay, thank you for that. What's the problem?"

"Well, this morning we had to make the decision to withdraw from the prison," said Derek.

The police officer frowned. "Withdraw? What do you mean, withdraw?"

"We had to withdraw all staff. The prisoners are now locked inside without supervision," said Derek bluntly.

The officers exchanged a glance, obviously shocked and confused by the statement, "Who's guarding them?"

"No one," said Derek. "Not until the army gets there."

"And when's that?"

"Soon, we hope," said Derek. "But the reason I need your help, is that I had to remove all the firearms from the prison before we left."

"I would hope so," said the driver sarcastically.

"I have them in my car," said Derek, gesturing over his shoulder. "I need to surrender them into storage."

The officer nodded.

"I tried a couple of different stations, but they were closed."

"Yeah, we're having serious staffing problems at the minute," said the driver. "Everyone's flat out."

"Can I give them to you to put in your station's armoury?"

The officers looked at each other again. Neither seemed comfortable with the idea.

"I'm sorry mate, that's not something we could do," said the officer.

"Do you have a gun safe at home?"

"Yes, but…"

"You'll need to just store them there until this's over," said the driver.

Derek tried to explain his situation further, but the closest cop stopped him with a raised hand as he and his partner focused on a voice in their ears. The driver turned and hurried back to the car without another word. His partner also started to move towards the car. "I'm sorry we have an emergency. You'll have to just keep them in your home safe. Sorry we couldn't help."

The officer trotted the last few feet and dropped into his seat. With blue lights now flashing, the car pulled away and accelerated hard, leaving a frustrated Derek standing at the roadside with his hands on his hips.

"For fuck's sake," he muttered, as he ambled back to his own car.

He continued on towards the city centre, but within another couple of streets, he pulled in again, much to Jenny's annoyance. He parked in a small lay-by at the front of Owens' grocery shop.

"I think Owens' is open," he said, nodding to the shutter on the front door, which was halfway up. "I might be able to get that Sudocrem and a few other things. There mightn't be any other shops open on the way."

He handed her the keys as he jumped from the car. "Keep the doors locked."

CHAPTER 24

Derek jogged towards the door of the shop, then slowed and stopped. There was a trail of footprints coming out through the door. They were painted in a thick, dark red liquid which faded with every step. It was blood.

Ducking under the shutter, Derek peered into the gloom of the small shop. After a couple of deliberate slow breaths, he took a cautious step inside and edged quietly along the first aisle. Within a couple of steps, his eyes adjusted to the low light, and he stopped abruptly, noticing something on the floor by the counter. His heart drummed in his chest. He'd feared the worst, and now he was witnessing it. Seamus Owens lay on his back, a pool of blood surrounding his motionless body, a figure looming over him, and a bloodied knife by his side.

Derek reached for his gun, his shaking hand unclipping it from its holster under his left arm. He'd never had reason to draw his personal protection weapon before and certainly had never pointed it at another living person.

"Don't you fucking move," he shouted, in a voice which caught in his throat.

The figure leaning over Seamus turned in a fright when he heard the words. The sight of the gun caused him to stumble as he recoiled.

Derek recognised the man. It took him a second to find the name within his racing thoughts, "Simon? What the fuck?"

"He's dead," stuttered Simon. "I found him like this."

Derek slowly lowered the gun. He instinctively knew, from Simon's reaction, from the bloody footprint and from a gut feeling, that Simon was not the perpetrator.

Seeing the gun being lowered, Simon regained his composure and stood.

"Is he definitely gone?" asked Derek, although from the scene in front of him, he knew the answer.

"Yes, I've checked, there's no pulse," said Simon, staring down at the body in a daze.

"Fuck."

"I'll phone the police," said Simon, rounding the counter and lifting the receiver of the phone mounted to the wall.

Derek stared down at Seamus. He'd seen plenty of dead bodies in the prison over the years, most by their own hand, and he'd seen even more knife wounds. He'd never seen anything like this. Seamus had been the victim of a frenzied attack. He had multiple wounds to his neck and his face, and cuts and slashes on his arms where he'd evidently tried in vain to ward off his attacker. The wooden club, which he kept for self-defence, lay by his side. It hadn't been enough in the end.

Derek felt light-headed. He needed some air; he needed to tell Jenny.

"I'll be back in a second," he said as he moved towards the door.

"You're not leaving, are you?" asked Simon in a panic, holding the phone away from his ear.

"No, my wife's in the car. I'll just be a minute."

Before Derek got to the door, a woman ducked under the shutter and straightened in front of him. She looked at him, at the gun which he still clutched in his hand, and then past him to the pool of blood which framed the shop owner's body. She let out an ear-piercing scream as she backed away and bolted out through the door.

The sound of the woman's scream seemed to catch Derek in his chest, and he suddenly felt the urge to retch. He re-holstered his gun and ducked through the door. The woman was gone. Jenny was now standing by her open car door. For the second time in a day, she saw a look on her husband's face that alarmed her.

"What happened? Why was that woman screaming?"

"Seamus Owens has been stabbed," said Derek as he approached.

"Oh my God."

"He's dead."

"Oh Jesus," cried Jenny, her words muffled in her cupped hands.

"Stay in the car. We're phoning the police."

"Who's we?"

"Another shopper, I know him, he's phoning them now," he looked nervously up and down the street. "Stay in the car. Please love and lock the doors."

Derek returned to the shop, pausing at the door for a couple of deep breaths before ducking back inside.

Simon looked relieved when he saw Derek return. "I'm still on hold," he said as Derek approached the counter again.

Derek looked down at the old shopkeeper lying at his feet. The right side of Seamus' face was awash with drying blood and his bushy white moustache was now dark and straight and slicked to his lip. His face was twisted in pain. His final moment must have been one of agony and fear. *The poor man*, thought Derek.

Carefully stepping around the body, he reached for an apron which hung on a hook beside the counter. The sweet metallic scent of fresh blood filled the air and blended with the sickly smell of detergent from an upturned mop bucket. The mixture threatened to stir Derek's stomach again. He draped the apron over Seamus and stood. It only covered the top half of his body, but it afforded him some measure of dignity.

Derek heard Simon speak into the phone. He'd finally got through to the police and was explaining the situation. He explained who he was, what he'd found, that Seamus was beyond saving and the fact that Derek was there with him.

Simon covered the phone with his hand. "Are you a cop Derek?" he whispered.

"No," said Derek, shaking his head but giving no further explanation for having a gun.

Simon frowned, but added nothing to the account he was giving the operator. After a series of *Okays* and verbal nods, Simon hung up the phone.

"What'd they say?" asked Derek.

"They said they'd send someone, but it could be some time. They're very stretched."

The two men stood in silence, looking down at the scene.

Simon shook his head slowly and released a long sorrowful sigh. "He was such a nice man."

"Yeah," said Derek, mirroring Simon's actions. "He should've stayed closed, for fuck's sake."

"He wanted to serve his community. That's just the way he was," said Simon.

Derek nodded.

"What do we do now?"

"I don't know. I've my wife and baby in the car outside."

"Shit. Did you tell her?"

"Yeah."

"How long do you think it'll take for the cops to get here?"

A sudden clanging, ratcheting roar startled the two, and they spun to face the door. The roller shutter had been flung up the rest of the way. A man and woman stepped into the doorway, silhouetted by the bright daylight behind them.

"The shop's closed," said Derek.

"It's an emergency," said the woman.

"I'm sorry you'll have to go somewhere else."

"There is nowhere else," said the man defiantly, as he stepped past his wife and into the shop. He stopped after two steps and froze.

"There's been an incident," said Derek. "You can't come in. The police are on their way."

The man backed away, then turned and ushered his wife forcefully from the shop. "Go, go, get out."

Another silhouette appeared and poked his head in, then another. Derek moved towards the door. "The shop's closed."

He thought of pulling the shutter back down, but he didn't want to create a separation between him and his family in the car. He reassured Jenny with a wave from the doorway. A crowd was starting to assemble in a small semi-circle around the front door of the shop.

Derek stepped back inside. "I don't know what to do here. There's a crowd gathering. I can't leave my wife sitting out there in the car much longer."

Simon rubbed at his chin. "We need to wait for the police."

"I know."

The light from the doorway was blocked momentarily, causing Derek to turn again. A large figure stepped purposely through the door.

"The shop's closed," said Derek in a commanding voice. "There's been a murder."

The big man in the doorway said nothing. He moved further into the shop, his focus moving between Derek and the gruesome scene beyond him, then slowly back to Derek. His eyes remained on Derek as he moved slowly sideways into the shop.

"Did you fucking hear me? The owner's been stabbed. He's dead. Get the fuck out," said Derek, taking a step towards the man. The man reared up, a claw hammer now raised and ready to strike. Still, he said nothing.

Derek edged backwards and put his hand on the grip of the gun under his arm, but he didn't draw it. He'd done so many things today already that could land him in jail. How many more would there be?

The man didn't follow Derek's retreat, instead his eyes darted to the items on the shelves, but then quickly back to Derek and then Simon. He moved slowly towards the items that he wanted, the hammer still raised and ready to strike. He was determined to get want he came for.

As he moved further into the shop, the man begin lifting items from the shelves and placing them in a canvas bag that hung awkwardly from the shoulder of his raised right arm.

Simon bent slowly and lifted the wooden cudgel that lay by Seamus's side.

"You can't fuckin' do this," said Simon. "The police will be here any second."

Behind the man, a couple of people edged their way into the shop. The man turned to assess the threat. Everyone moved in slow motion. More people slipped through the door and cautiously, silently infiltrated the store, careful to keep out of arm's length of the hammer welding shopper.

Derek glanced at Simon, a worried look on his face.

Seeing the newcomers more as an affirmation of his actions than any kind of threat, the big man began to move with more purpose. He moved away from Derek, further into the store and even lowered his weapon, allowing him to loot with more efficiency. The doorway was now clear, apart from the trickle of new looters tentatively entering.

Derek looked to Simon. "We can't stay here."

"We can't just leave Seamus lying here," said Simon in weak protest.

"Well, we can't take him with us," barked Derek, "and there's nothing we can do about these fuckers."

Simon looked nervously at the growing swarm of looters frantically snapping at Seamus's neatly stacked shelves.

"I can't leave my wife sitting out there with this going on," shouted Derek as he moved towards the door. "Are you coming?"

Simon looked down and Seamus's body and hesitated, then with one last prompt from Derek he thawed his feet from the floor and bolted after him.

The two men had to push their way through the growing mob at the door and out into the sunlight.

Derek emerged from the crowd and saw his wife's terror-filled face framed in the car window.

"Get in the car!" shouted Derek.

Simon rounded the car and climbed into the back seat, pushing bags and blankets aside to make room, careful not to disturb the tiny baby sleeping in the car-seat beside him.

Derek started the car and pulled out, the now stereotypical looting scene playing out in his rear-view mirror as he accelerated away. He stopped and let the car idle at the end of the street, and all three turned in their seats to look back at the scene.

"What the hell just happened?" said Simon.

"Fuckin' animals," said Derek, his heart was thumping in his chest. He was spooked. What if the mob had have turned on Jenny in the car?

The car was silent for a long moment, each of them trying to process what they'd just seen.

Simon looked down at the heavy wooden club lying across his lap, and at the streak of blood along one side which had now transferred to his jeans.

"What do we do now?" he asked. "The police are expecting us to be there."

"Nothing we can do about that now," said Derek. "Is there somewhere we can leave you?"

"I live a few streets away," said Simon. "Turn right here."

###

Simon stared vacantly at the back of Derek's headrest. He was numb. The adrenaline and nervous energy had started to ebb from him, and fatigue was setting in. Behind his heavy eyelids, a fight was in progress as a myriad of thoughts demanded his attention and scrambled over each other to get it. His every sense sizzled towards overload, and to top it off, a sickly stench invaded his nostrils as the baby beside him announced the filling of a nappy with an ear-splitting incessant screech.

"Just here," he said, when the familiar sight of his apartment complex came into view.

Derek pulled alongside the curb.

"What are you gonna do now?" asked Simon.

"We need to go to the relief point at the City Hall."

"Don't bother," said Simon, "I was there an hour ago. It was chaos. I couldn't get anywhere near it."

"Really?" asked Derek, turning in his seat.

"Yeah, I'd say there were tens of thousands trying to get through."

Derek exchanged a look of concern with his wife, who was reaching back and trying to soothe the baby.

"Listen, you're welcome to come up to my apartment," said Simon. "I gave the cops my address. They might come here after they go to Seamus's shop."

"I'd be surprised if you hear from them at all until this's all over," said Derek.

"Why don't you come in for a while anyway until you work out what you're gonna do?" said Simon. He really didn't want to be alone.

Derek's wife seemed keen on the idea and urged Derek with her eyes.

"I don't know," said Derek. He looked at the gates into the carpark. "Do those gates open?"

"Yes, we've a battery hooked up to open them," said Simon, a little too keen.

"I'll need to feed the baby soon, so it might not be a bad idea," said Derek's wife.

"Okay," said Derek.

"Right, I'll open the gates."

Simon got out of the car and jogged to the pedestrian gate, which was still ajar. He closed it behind him and dragged the plastic storage box containing the car battery over to the control unit for the main gates. He'd seen Eugene connect it a couple of times now, so he was able to hook it up quickly, and when he heard the familiar buzz, he pulled the double gates open with ease to let Derek drive through.

Simon pushed the large gates closed and disconnected the battery before sealing it again in the waterproof box.

Derek parked the car and lifted a bulky baby bag from the boot. His wife was unstrapping their son from his car seat.

"Do you need a hand with anything?" asked Simon. "I'm sorry, but I'm on the fifth floor."

"Yeah thanks, would you mind taking this?" said Derek handing him the baby bag.

"Sure," said Simon.

"I'm Jenny, by the way," said Jenny with a brief smile, as she approached, cradling the baby.

"Sorry. Simon," he said, returning the smile.

Derek finished at the boot and came away with a large, green duffel bag. It didn't seem to be full to capacity, but its contents strained against the fabric at various angles, and the way Derek hefted it, it looked heavy.

"Do you need a hand with that?"

"No, it's fine. I've got it," said Derek a little sharply.

Simon led them up the five flights of stairs to his apartment. He was happy to be in the safety of his own home.

"I need to feed the baby," said Jenny.

"There's a bedroom just at the end of the hall," said Simon, not sure if she was asking for somewhere private or just giving him a heads-up.

"Thank you."

"I'm gonna boil some water for coffee. Would you like some Jenny?" asked Simon.

"Yes, that'd be great Simon, thank you, actually would you have any tea?"

"Sure. Derek?"

"Yeah, coffee would be good, thanks," said Derek, taking a seat on the long sofa and setting the canvas bag beside him.

Simon's hands trembled as he filled a saucepan from his last remaining five-litre bottle of water and set it on the camping stove. He couldn't get Seamus' face out of his mind. *Animals*, he thought.

"It might be a few minutes. This thing takes ages to heat."

"That's fine, I haven't had a coffee all week. That's handy," said Derek, nodding at the camp stove.

Simon lowered himself into the chair opposite Derek. The two men stared at the floor, the silence punctuated by the occasional deep sigh.

"I can't believe this is happening. Poor Seamus," said Simon.

"I know," said Derek, shaking his head slowly.

"Do you think it was those guys he was arguing with on Tuesday?"

Derek shrugged. "Could've been them, or someone else like them who was just desperate."

"Did you notice that he had his cudgel?"

"Yeah, I saw that. He must've been trying to force them to leave."

There was another period of silence.

"Have you ever seen a dead body before?" asked Simon, eventually.

"Yeah, unfortunately," said Derek. "You?"

"That's the second one this week," said Simon. "I found my elderly neighbour trapped in the lift on Monday morning. She died in there, in the middle of the night."

"Fuck, that's terrible. Being stuck in the dark on her own, it must've been terrifying."

"Her teenage granddaughter was in there with her."

"Oh shit," said Derek. He pressed his palm to his face. "Poor girl."

"Yeah, we got her out, but we had to wait for the Fire and Rescue guys to get Janet out. I'll never forget them hoisting her out. Jesus, it was awful."

"It never gets easy."

They sat quietly again, each in their own thoughts.

Simon was curious. He wanted to know what Derek's profession was. He had a gun but wasn't a cop, and now he was saying that Seamus wasn't the first dead body he'd seen. Army? Maybe he should've found out before inviting him into his home. *And what's with the bag?* Simon thought. He was starting to feel a little uneasy.

"I can't believe how quickly things turned back there," said Derek.

"Yeah, it was madness," agreed Simon. "Mob mentality. I could really feel the tension in the crowd down at City Hall, too."

"Yeah? What was happening? Were the army there?"

"Yes, but they seemed to have lost control," said Simon. "Are you in the army?"

"No," said Derek flatly.

Simon said nothing. He waited for Derek to continue, to explain why he had a gun.

"Shit, the water's boiling over," said Derek, pointing to the kitchen.

CHAPTER 25

Lisa and Martin pulled into the staff car park. The barrier at the gate had been left open, the security guard seemingly the latest absentee.

As they approached the front door, Lisa saw Barry leaning against a small wall a few feet from the door. The spot was used as the designated smoking area for staff. Barry looked broken, his clothes were dishevelled, he had rough stubble and his hair... ugh; it made Lisa think of a slicked seagull after an oil spillage.

He sucked nervously at a cigarette and starred vacantly at the ground in front of him. He turned and watched them approach, expressionless.

"Hi Barry," said Lisa.

"Hey."

"Any further update from the team?" asked Lisa.

Barry snorted, "Ha, what team? This is it. Everyone else is gone."

"Gone?" said Lisa, only half surprised. She winced as a lungful of rancid cigarette smoke incited a sudden bout of heartburn.

"Yeah, they said they needed to be with their families, and needed to go and try to get food at the relief stations."

Lisa said nothing and just shook her head. She understood. If she had a family to support, she was sure she'd be doing the same.

"How'd it go at City Hall?" asked Barry.

"It started off fine," said Lisa. Martin nodded beside her, "but it was getting a bit crazy when we left."

"They just didn't have enough troops to control the crowds," said Martin.

"Why? How many people turned up?" asked Barry.

"There was a steady flow for the first hour or so and then it just went nuts," said Lisa.

"I'd say there were a few thousand within a couple of hours," added Martin.

"How many can they handle?" asked Barry.

"They had supplies for about five thousand," said Lisa glumly.

"They said they'd have more tomorrow, but the officer in charge didn't know how he was gonna manage the distribution with the few men he had," said Martin.

Barry sighed and shook his head while taking the final wet draw from his cigarette.

"There's another problem," said Lisa, reluctant to add to Barry's woes. "The two radio stations we were at say they only have enough generator fuel to get through another day or so."

Barry didn't react. Bad news just washed over him at this stage. He stubbed his cigarette out and turned to Martin. "Martin, thank you for everything you've done this week. I'm sorry we didn't listen to you sooner."

"I'm not sure I was much help," said Martin, "and I don't think a couple of hours' warning would really have made much difference in the end."

"Maybe, maybe not," said Barry.

"So what now?" asked Lisa.

"I think that's all we can do," said Barry. "In terms of our remit, we've given all the advice we can. It's over to the politicians and the army now."

He may have been a bit of a prick and a hapless boss, but at least he was dedicated. He stuck around and did his best, which was more than could be said for most of the rest.

"I'd suggest you go home and try to ride this out," said Barry. "God knows how long that'll be, though."

Barry turned to Lisa, "And Lisa, thank you for all your hard work. You really stepped up, and went above and beyond. Assuming things get back to normal, you'll have a glowing review from me."

Lisa smiled. "Just doing my job, but thank you, Barry."

"Okay, you two take care," said Barry as he headed for the door.

Martin squinted as he watched Barry disappear through the main door, the orange reflection from the retreating sun rebounding off the glass fronted building.

"So what'll you do now, Lisa?" said Martin. He'd spend most of the week with her, but he realised he knew very little about her situation. "Do you have family here?"

"No, my parents live up in Donegal," said Lisa. "My brother lives in Belfast, but he was due to finish work yesterday and was heading up home."

"Would he still have been working? Would his place have been able to open?"

"The whole idea is that it doesn't open," said Lisa with a smile.

Martin tilted his head inquisitively.

"He's a prison officer."

"Ah right," said Martin. He hadn't considered the impact on prisons. How long could they hold out for without power?

His thoughts must've etched a frown on his face, which Lisa reacted too. "Why? What's the problem with that?"

"No nothing, I was just wondering how long a prison is designed to operate for without power," said Martin. "It was something I hadn't thought of."

"I spoke to Ray on Sunday evening before the power cut," said Lisa. "I told him to expect it. Maybe they would've been able to put some things in place."

"That's if he believed you," said Martin with an ironic smile.

Lisa raised her eyebrows and smiled.

"Are you going up to your parents too, then?" asked Martin.

"Yeah, but I think I'll wait until the morning. I've to head home and pack some stuff, and I don't want to drive up in the dark."

Martin bobbed his head.

"What about you? Do you have family here, other than Simon?"

"No, Simon's not family," said Martin.

"Oh, sorry, I assumed you were a couple," said Lisa. "I'm sorry."

Martin felt his face and neck flush instantly. "No, what gave you that idea?" he said with a nervous laugh and an exaggerated frown. "Simon was married. He lost his wife a couple of years ago in a car crash."

"Oh right, that's terrible."

"We're just friends. He's coming with me to Fermanagh. My family has a house down there," said Martin. "My mum, and my brother and his family will be there."

"And will you have enough supplies?"

"Yeah, I got a pile of stuff on Sunday," he said, pointing to his car which was parked beside hers. "Should last us a few weeks, and my brother's into fishing, so that should keep us going too."

"Sounds like you've got it well planned out."

"It has solar panels too," he said with a smile.

"You're just showing off now."

Martin laughed, yeah he probably was.

"How long do you really think this'll last, Martin?"

"I don't know. I actually thought some of my warnings were worst-case scenario, but you can see, I wasn't that far off."

"Yeah, and that's scary."

"Every day that goes by, people are going to become more and more desperate," said Martin. "Just look at how crazy it got at City Hall today. Can you imagine what tomorrow's going to be like?"

"I know. I wouldn't want to be in that Captain's boots."

They stood for a moment in silence, watching the sky slowly change colour. This time it was from the setting sun and not from a world changing solar storm.

"So, when this's all over, we'll have to meet up for a drink," said Lisa. "You can bring your friend Simon too if you like."

"Yeah, I'd like that."

"I'm gonna grab my stuff and hit the road," said Lisa.

"Yeah, I've some things to get too."

They walked back to the STAC office for the last time to collect their belongings and go their separate ways.

CHAPTER 26

Derek was grateful for the hot coffee, his first in four days. With a long slow inhale, he savoured the calming, nut-like, carmelly aroma. A couple of tiny white specks floated to the edge of the cup. The milk was past its best, but it was still great. Of all the inconveniences since the power had gone off, not being able to have his morning coffee had been the worst, then he reminded himself of the fact that he'd just locked 900 men in a cage, so maybe a lack of coffee wasn't the worst thing.

He rested his elbows on his knees and ran his hand slowly through his hair. He noticed Simon staring at the kit bag sitting beside him on the chair. He should probably explain why he was carrying a gun.

Caution and secrecy about his profession had been drummed into him since he first applied to the prison service. His first thought had to be for his safety and that of his family. It was a hard habit to break.

"I'm a prison officer, by the way," he said.

"Ah, ok," said Simon nonchalantly, as if he wasn't fixated on the question.

"That's why I'm carrying a gun," said Derek, moving his left arm to expose the holstered weapon. "It's my personal protection weapon."

"I didn't know prison officers were armed."

"We can request one if we think we need it for safety."

"What prison do you work in? If you don't mind me asking?"

"Maghaberry."

"And how's the power cut affecting them? I suppose everything runs on generators?"

"Yeah, most stuff," said Derek. He didn't want to get into the whole story. This guy was still a stranger, after all.

Derek was relieved when Jenny came in. The baby was asleep in the baby carrier. He lifted the kit bag from the seat beside him and Jenny took its place, setting the carrier on the floor by her feet.

Derek noticed Simon looking questioningly at the bulky bag, which clanged a little when he set it down.

Simon went to the kitchen and came back with Jenny's tea. "The milk isn't the freshest, I'm afraid."

"I'm sure it'll be fine, thank you," said Jenny.

"The milk's fine, it's just nice to have a warm drink," said Derek. "Our cooker's electric so we haven't even been able to boil water."

"You've gas, do you?" asked Jenny.

"Yeah, but it stopped working, too. Apparently, it's pumped by an electric pump in the basement. I've been using that wee camping stove."

"Ah, very good," said Jenny, taking a sip. "Well, it does the job."

There was an awkward lull in the small talk as the three sat sipping their drinks.

"It's a wee boy, is it?" asked Simon.

"Yes," said Derek, looking proudly at his son.

"How old?"

"Just over two weeks," said Jenny.

"Whoa, he's big for two weeks," said Simon, raising his eyebrows. "I'm sure this power cut was the last thing you needed."

The two new parents nodded.

"So how do you two know each other?" asked Jenny.

"We don't really," said Derek with a smile. "Just from going to Owen's."

"We've bumped into each other a couple of times this week," said Simon. "I'm glad you recognised me and didn't shoot me."

"Shoot you?" exclaimed Jenny, staring at Derek. "What's that mean?"

"I thought he was attacking Seamus. I drew my gun."

"You what?" said Jenny incredulously. "What the hell happened in there?"

Between them, Derek and Simon recanted the events in the shop and the room fell silent again, as the image of Seamus returned to them.

"Simon knows Ray's sister," he said to Jenny. "Lisa," he clarified to Simon.

"Well, I don't *know* her. I've only met her once," said Simon. "My friend has been helping her this week."

"The professor," said Derek.

"Ah," said Jenny, "I've heard him on the radio with her. He knew this was coming, did he?"

"Only from Sunday morning," said Simon. "He tried to warn people, but they wouldn't listen."

Jenny shook her head slowly.

"He should be here any time, actually," said Simon. "He's a place in Fermanagh. We're heading there as soon as he's finished helping Lisa and her team."

"Where are you from originally, Simon?" asked Jenny.

"The south of England, but I've lived here for about fifteen years, since college," said Simon.

"Do you have family here?" she asked.

"No, not anymore." Simon took a sip of his coffee. "My wife died a couple of years ago."

"Oh, I'm sorry," said Jenny with a sympathetic smile.

"What about you guys? Are you going somewhere too?"

"We're supposed to be going to Donegal," said Jenny, looking at Derek.

"But we can't go yet," said Derek. He looked at the bag of weapons sitting at his feet. He'd noticed Simon looking at it a few times. It'd become the elephant in the room.

This guy had invited them into his home. After they shared a harrowing experience, I should probably be straight with him, thought Derek.

"I can't go over the border with firearms," he said.

"Firearms?" asked Simon, emphasising the S.

"Yeah," Derek gestured to the bag, "I've others from the prison that I need to surrender to the police or army before we go."

Simon frowned deeply. "I don't understand. Why are they not in the prison?"

Derek looked at Jenny, who looked back at him supportively. "We had to close the prison."

Simon's frown grew deeper still. "How do they close a prison? Did they just let the prisoners out?"

"No," said Derek. He was regretting saying anything. They shouldn't have even come into this man's home. "We didn't have enough staff, so we had to withdraw from the prison. The army will be going in over the next couple of days to take over."

I hope, thought Derek.

He could feel his anxiety rise. Verbalising what they'd done, what *he* had done, was making it seem more and more like a mistake; inhumane, barbaric.

"So the prisoners are just locked in with no one guarding them?" asked Simon.

Derek nodded and looked at Jenny, who took his hand and squeezed it.

"Jesus, what idiot made that decision?"

"Me."

"Oh," said Simon, wide-eyed.

Silence descended again as the two men looked anywhere but at each other.

"Do you mind if I use your bathroom?" asked Derek. He needed to get out of the room.

"Ah yeah sure, but the water isn't running, so you'll have to fill the cistern with water from the bath so that you can flush it."

"Oh, ok."

"There's a bucket in there."

###

"I'm sorry," said Simon, when Derek had left the room. "I hope I didn't offend him?"

Jenny shook her head. "He's beating himself up about the decision to abandon the prison," she said in a hushed tone.

"Yeah, I'm sure," said Simon.

"But he had no choice. They didn't have enough staff and he couldn't get in contact with anyone in the Department of Justice."

Simon shook his head.

"And the governor just fucked off and left them on Tuesday," she said bitterly.

"Seriously?"

"Yeah. So Derek was left to make the decision."

"My God."

"And the police and army basically said they were on their own," said Jenny. "They said they didn't have anyone to spare."

"But the army will be going in to take over at the weekend?" said Simon.

"That's what Derek's hoping."

Simon raised his eyebrows and scratched his head. He couldn't imagine the stress of having to make a decision like that.

"And now he won't go over the border until he's surrendered these bloody guns," said Jenny, pointing at the bag on the floor.

"Can he not just leave them into a police station or something?"

"I tried that," said Derek, appearing at the door and not looking happy about being talked about. "The two stations I tried were closed. There was literally no one there."

"Right," said Simon, a little embarrassed at having been caught talking about him behind his back. "So that's why you need to go to the army relief point?"

"Yeah," said Derek, as he took his seat again beside his wife, to whom he shot a stern look.

"I don't think you'll get near the City Hall one. It was bedlam when I was there and the crowds were still growing."

"Yeah, the one at Lisburn was the same," said Derek.

"You might have better luck at one of the stations out in the country," said Simon.

"Possibly, but I don't have enough petrol to be driving all over the place looking for one that's open," said Derek.

He looked like a man at the end of his tether, like one more setback would put him over the edge.

"You might have a better chance in the morning," said Simon.

Derek nodded, and Jenny gave him a worried look.

"We really wanted to be on the road today. We don't want to have to go back home," said Derek.

"The streets are getting a bit crazy round our way," said Jenny.

"Well, you're welcome to stay here tonight if you like, and try in the morning," Simon said. "To be honest, I'd welcome the company. I'm still a bit rattled after… after what happened to Seamus."

Jenny looked at Derek.

"Really, there's plenty of room," said Simon.

"Thank you, Simon, but we wouldn't want to impose," said Derek.

"It might be a good idea," said Jenny, urging her husband to accept.

"Well, it's up to you," said Simon. "I really don't mind."

Derek considered it for a moment. "Well, if you really don't mind, then that might actually be a good idea. Are you sure now?"

"Yes, it's not a problem at all," said Simon.

"You can take that back bedroom. It has an en suite," he added, pointing down the hall. "Although you'll need to do the same thing with the cistern to use the toilet."

"Sure."

"On second thoughts, it might be better for you to take the smaller room if you don't mind," said Simon. "I need to keep the balcony door in there open so that I can hear Martin's horn when he comes."

"Yes, any room will be fine, thank you Simon," said Derek. "Actually talking about the toilet, there wasn't much water left in your bath."

"Right, okay," said Simon, thinking about what other options they might have. "You know what we could do. If we had a rope, we could use the bucket and get water from the river out the back."

Derek laughed. "Yeah, I suppose that'd work."

Simon rubbed the back of his neck. "I think the only rope I have is in my car which is stuck in the garage with the roller shutter down."

"I think I've a tow rope in the car," said Derek.

Jenny smiled, "It's turning into a real operation, this."

"Well, you'll be thankful when you need to use the toilet," said Derek with a smile.

"Jez, who thought we'd have third world problems like this," said Jenny. "Having to fetch water with a bucket."

"Could be the new norm," said Simon.

"I'll go down and get the rope," said Derek.

"Sure, I'll come with you and bring the bucket, and we can give it a go," said Simon. "Are you okay there, Jenny?"

"Yes, I'll be fine."

"There's a wee wind up radio there," said Simon, pointing to the shelf. "If you don't mind risking RSI to wind the thing up."

"Yeah, okay, thanks."

###

Derek's thighs burned. He and Simon had done five runs to the river, each time adding another bucketful of smelly brown water to the bath. It looked like someone had just washed a mud-caked St. Bernard.

At least this time they weren't lugging the heavy bucket of water. The flimsy metal handle had finally given way as they tried to haul it out of the river for the last time. Derek felt guilty. Maybe he'd filled it too much, or had pulled too hard when he was trying to raise it up. Either way, it was now gone, and they'd have to make do with the water they'd managed to collect.

He could see that Simon was also struggling with the last few flights. "Are you okay there?" asked Derek.

"Ha, yeah," said Simon breathlessly, "I knew I was out of shape, but I didn't think I was this bad."

They finally reached the apartment door. As Simon opened it, he stopped abruptly, as if slapped in the face. Derek soon realised what'd hit him. It was a toxic, nuclear stench that Derek still hadn't acclimatised to, even after two weeks.

Derek smiled to himself when he saw the look on Simon's face. "Sorry Simon, looks like my son has christened your apartment."

"Ah, don't worry about it," said Simon with a laugh, although he nearly choked when he spoke.

"Do you mind if I have a cigarette out on your balcony?"

"No, go ahead," said Simon. "I might join you, but I think I need a drink, you want one."

"Yeah, that would be great. What have you?"

"Gin and coke is all I've left."

"Yeah, sounds good."

"What about Jenny?" asked Simon. She must've been in the bedroom with the baby.

"No, she's fine. She can't drink while she's breastfeeding and she'll not thank you for reminding her," said Derek with a smile.

The two men crowded on to the small balcony. Darkness was creeping in, soon the only light would be from the near-full moon.

Derek tilted the cigarette pack towards Simon. "Smoke?"

"I don't, but if you don't mind, I will steal one," said Simon.

Derek half expected him just to break it in two and stick a half up each nostril.

Derek drew hard on his cigarette. The hit of nicotine had an immediate relaxing effect, although the smoke stung his lungs, which were still burning from the stair climbing. Simon coughed and spluttered the way non-smokers do on their occasional cigarette.

"I keep meaning to give these up," said Derek.

Simon smiled sympathetically. "Today's not the day, though?"

"Nope."

"Jesus, what a day," said Simon, with a sigh that turned into another cough.

"Yeah. Are you okay?"

"Not really," said Simon. "I thought seeing Janet was bad, but Seamus." He shook his head and took a long drink of his gin.

"What do you think'll happen with the prison?" ask Simon.

"I don't know. I just hope the army move in soon."

"What happens if they don't?"

Derek closed his eyes and shook his head. He didn't want to talk about it; he didn't want to think about what could be going on behind those locked gates. But Simon seemed to be in a chatty mood, maybe trying to distract himself from his own thoughts.

"What'll you do in the morning if you can't find someone to take your guns?" asked Simon.

Jesus stop with the questions will you, thought Derek, I don't fucking know.

"I'll go back to the prison and see if the army's arrived yet," said Derek.

"And if they're not there? Do you not think under the circumstances the authorities would understand if you had to bring them with you?" asked Simon.

Derek took another draw on his cigarette and squinted at Simon through the smoke. "Taking them over the border is not an option, under any circumstances," he said sharply. *Is this guy a fucking idiot?*

In truth, he'd no idea what he'd do if he couldn't hand them in somewhere. It would be just his luck that he'd step over the border with a bag full of British guns and the lights would suddenly come back on. Add *International Incident* to his growing list of offences.

"Well, if you were stuck, I'm sure Martin wouldn't mind if you came with us to Fermanagh for a couple of days. His place sleeps about twelve," said Simon.

"Well, we'll see in the morning. Your mate might not be happy with you inviting more strangers along," he said with a smile.

"I'm sure he'd be fine, especially as you know Lisa," said Simon.

Simon stubbed his cigarette out. Not that he'd smoked much of it. "I've some pasta and a jar of Dolmio sauce, that okay for you and Jenny?"

"Ah, here, we don't want to be eating the last of your food."

"Don't worry, I've plenty of pasta and I'm opening the jar anyway," said Simon. "Plus, Martin should be here by tomorrow at the latest, I'd say."

"Okay, if you don't mind, that would be great."

Simon headed through to the kitchen. Derek stubbed his own cigarette out and followed him, pulling the sliding patio door closed behind him.

CHAPTER 27

"Here mate, can you spare any of that water you have there?"

Martin turned from the gate. Two ghostly figures stared out from under their hoods. Another stood by the rear window of his car, examining the stacked contents.

"I'm sorry no, I can't," said Martin, half turning towards the gate, longing for Simon to appear. He'd been shouting his name for ages. Where was he?

"He's got a whole pile of stuff in here," said the tall one by the car.

"I'm sorry guys, I can't spare anything. I'm just here to pick up my friend. He's on his way down now." He hoped.

Where are you Simon? He thought, fear rising as the two closest youths edged nearer.

"Look mate, we're fuckin' starvin'. You've tons of food in there," said the one with the abnormally big head, as he stepped closer still. His sidekick moved in too, his sunken eyes barely visible in the faint moonlight.

The tall one at the car moved to the driver's door and tugged at the handle. Disappointed, he turned and joined his friends as they slowly closed around Martin.

Martin backed away, back now against the gate with nowhere else to retreat to.

Where are you Simon? He pleaded silently for his friend to come to his rescue.

"Look just give us your keys mate," said the leader, with a tilt of his fat head and a shrug of his shoulders, suggesting that Martin should resign himself to the fact that there was nothing he could do to prevent them from taking everything.

"Will you just fuck off!" snapped Martin, all civility gone. "I'm not giving you anything. I need that for my family. Now piss off and leave me alone."

"Gimme the fucking keys now," screamed the leader, transforming instantly from cheeky chancer to menacing psychopath.

A surge of adrenaline spurred Martin into action. He wasn't a fighter. He'd never thrown a punch in his life. Stepping forward, he shoved the leader back.

"Get away from me," he screamed.

Without a word or hint of emotion, the taller youth rushed in. He pinned Martin against the gate with his left forearm and punched him in the stomach.

The wind rushed from Martin's lungs as his attacker pulled back; the moonlight glinting off a knife in his hand. It wasn't just a punch. Terror filled Martin as the searing pain gripped him and the realisation dawned.

Fuck, he stabbed me, he thought. He clutched at his belly and looked in horror at a warm wet patch spreading across his favourite shirt.

"Simon!" Martin screamed. "Okay, stop, stop."

The first attacker hesitated just long enough for his two friends to step in, their own blades now clasped tightly. Like their friend, their faces were void of emotion. This wasn't an act of hatred, it was just a necessity.

Martin reached out, trying to fend off the blows that came in rapid succession. Each short, sharp jab burned.

The pain spasmed through him like the sting of a thousand bees. Even as he crumpled and slid down against the gate, the flurry of stabs and slices kept coming. His stomach, his sides, his arms, his hands. The frenzied attack was relentless.

"Get his fucking keys, Cheesey," shouted one of the attackers.

His first attacker stepped in again as the other two ceased, tired from their brutal exertion. Martin could no longer raise his arms to defend himself. He lay twisted and broken, his arms wrapped across his torn body. The thug knelt and leaned in close, Martin smelt the putrid stench from the yellow and black patchwork of teeth, the dead eyes showing no compassion as he patted at Martin's pockets, pulling him roughly to the side to reach into his left jacket pocket where he'd felt the protruding car keys.

Without a word, the three backed away, the tall one taking the driver's seat while the other two squeezed together into the passenger seat.

Martin watched as his car reversed away from the gate, paused, lurched forward, and then screeched away into the night. The whole scene shown crimson when the taillights briefly washed over him as he lay in the spreading pool of blood.

Beyond the cramping, spasming pain, Martin could feel the warmth spread across his torso, but he was cold, so cold. His face pressed against the iron bars of the gate, distorting his features. His glasses lay cracked and twisted by his side.

"Simon," he croaked, no more than a whisper.

"Martin," cried Simon, skidding to his knees on the other side of the gate. "Jesus, oh fuck. I'm here Martin, you're gonna to be alright. Just hold on."

Martin turned his eyes slowly to see his friend, no longer having the strength to lift his head.

"Someone help me here," Simon screamed, looking around for assistance. "Get this fuckin' gate open quick. Hurry up!"

Behind him, Derek and Eugene wrestled with the car battery and began connecting it to the gate controls.

Simon cradled his friend's head through the bars of the gate with his left hand and pressed his right on top of Martin's, to put pressure on the wounds.

Martin stared at his only friend. In a cruel world, Simon was the only person who'd ever shown him kindness, who'd ever respected him. A tear rolled down his cheek.

"I'm scared Simon," he said. "I don't wanna die."

I love you Simon; he wanted to say, but he knew Simon didn't see their friendship that way.

"It's gonna be okay Martin," Simon said. "Get this gate open," he shouted over his shoulder.

"Simon... I'm scared," Martin breathed the words rather than saying them.

Eugene connected the red crocodile clip. The gate lock clicked and let out a long, slow buzz.

Martin heard the buzz behind the voices and shouts. It was faint and fading. Then it was gone.

CHAPTER 28

Simon edged backwards, still holding Martin's head through the gate, as Derek and Eugene opened it just enough to squeeze through. They eased Martin away from the swinging gate and laid him down flat.

Simon rounded the gate and joined the others as they applied pressure to the many knife wounds. It was obvious that Derek knew at least basic first aid as he took control. He tried to find a pulse. There wasn't one. He checked to see if Martin was breathing; he wasn't. Derek looked at Simon gravely. Simon pleaded for him to do something.

"We need to do CPR," cried Simon. "Quickly!"

As Derek started CPR, Simon and Eugene tried to make space while still holding the worst of the cuts on Martin's body. There was so much blood. Martin's torso was saturated, as were the trouser legs of the three men trying to help him as they knelt in the expanding puddle of blood.

"We need to phone an ambulance," said Simon in a panic. "Eugene, go and use Janet's phone? Kick the door in if you have to."

Eugene hesitated for a second, then got up and sprinted back towards the apartment block. Simon tried to cover the wounds that Eugene had been keeping pressure on.

Derek continued to alternate between the kiss of life and chest compressions. He seemed to know what he was doing, but Martin wasn't responding. Derek looked at Simon briefly, expressionless.

Simon felt hot tears roll down his cheeks. He twisted awkwardly to wipe them away with his shoulder. He hadn't noticed the other neighbours gathering behind him until he heard the murmurs and gasps. His hands were warm and slick with his friend's blood. The same metallic, iron smell from Seamus' shop filled his nostrils.

Derek looked at Simon, a stern, sorrowful frown, but he kept going. Then he slowed. Then he stopped. He sat back on his heels, exhausted, defeated.

"No. Derek, don't stop."

"I'm sorry Simon, he's gone. There's nothing we can do. He's lost too much blood."

Simon knew he was right, there was just too much blood.

He cradled his friend's head in his arms and cursed the cruel world that had abused and bullied him, had ridiculed and laughed at him, and now, when he'd done all he could to help, they took all he had left, including his life. Because they could.

Derek stood in his shorts at the bathroom sink, his blood-soaked clothes lying in a pile behind him. His legs, from his knees down, were stained like red wine spilt on a tablecloth.

He leaned heavily on the sink and starred at his reflection in the mirror. The light from the single candle cast a haunting image. He was physically and emotionally exhausted, and the trauma of the day was etched on his face.

He scrubbed at his skin, from his fingers to his elbows, with the little water they had. He even used the murky river water from the bath to try to rinse the worst of the blood away. Baby wipes got them to an acceptable state.

He dressed in fresh clothes and cleaned the sink as best he could. Simon would need to do the same at some stage, when they could get him to move from the kitchen table where he'd been slumped since the ambulance had finally taken his friend's body away.

Before today, Derek had barely known the guy whose home he and his family were now guests in. Two gruesome murders later, and he now felt an odd kinship. He guessed they were both experiencing the worst days of their lives.

Jenny met Derek outside the bathroom. She was showing surprising strength and resolve, given the events of the day. Derek was usually so calm and confident under pressure, but he knew without Jenny, he would've fallen to pieces. Together, they would have to help their new friend.

"Are you okay?" asked Jenny quietly.

"Yeah," said Derek with a sigh. "How's he doing?"

"He hasn't said a word. I think he's in shock. We need to try to get him cleaned up."

Derek nodded. "We need to get him something with plenty of sugar in it."

"What'd the police say?"

"There were only two of them," said Derek. "It was crazy. They took pictures on their phones and took statements from us, and that was it. They were away within half an hour."

"Seriously? For a murder?"

"They said they'd follow up when the power was back on and they were back to full strength. They said the city was going nuts; looting everywhere, riots and paramilitaries controlling various areas."

Jenny was visibly shaken. "What are we gonna do, Derek?"

"I'm not sure yet, but going home isn't an option."

"We can't expect to go with Simon to Fermanagh now," said Jenny. "What would we do, turn up and say, sorry, your son, who we didn't know, is dead but can we stay here?"

"I know. Let's try to get Simon sorted out first and then we can work it out," said Derek, as he made his way through to the kitchen.

"Hey mate, how you holding up?" said Derek.

Simon sat at the table, staring glassy-eyed at his blood-stained hands.

"I'll make you some tea," said Derek, when he got no reaction from Simon.

"We should try to get you cleaned, Simon," said Jenny.

"He went out of his way to try to help," said Simon quietly.

Jenny nodded.

Simon rubbed his eye on his bicep. "We could've been away days ago, but he stayed to help."

"Yeah, sounds like he was a good guy," said Derek.

Simon turned to him. "Did you see who it was? It was those fucking junkies I bet you."

"No, I didn't see them. When I heard your name being called, I looked out from the balcony and just saw the car speeding off."

"I fuckin' know it was them." Simon's eyes now burned with rage.

"There's a lot of desperate people out there. We saw that earlier," said Derek.

"He was a good guy. He wouldn't have hurt a fly," said Simon.

"Let me help you get cleaned up Simon, come on," said Jenny, and she ushered him into the bathroom.

With her bags now wedged in on top of the supplies she'd bought, at Martin's advice, Lisa closed the boot of her car. *Thanks, Martin,* she thought.

She glanced along the street. One or two other households were busy packing their cars, also keen to get out of the city. A few people stood in conversation with neighbours at their gates or over adjoining fences, likely exchanging hand-wringing accounts of disturbing events from the previous days.

Lisa was sure there would be many such accounts. She'd witnessed some herself. On the short drive home the previous night, she'd seen at least three shops looted, one still in progress. The police were even present at that one, but had to just sit back and watch, powerless against the sheer number of frenzied looters.

She couldn't blame people. If they weren't able to get food anywhere else, then it was inevitable that they'd take matters into their own hands eventually, but so soon? It'd only been four full days.

She felt a pang of guilt. Maybe she could've done more. Maybe if the army had have been called in sooner? If only the decision makers had have listened to people like Martin from the start?

She pushed the notion of guilt away; it wasn't reasonable to expect everyone to jump into action on day-one; it was a bloody power cut for God's sake, power cuts are always fixed within a day or two. Why would they have thought any differently this time?

She'd done all she could. It was time to think of herself and her family. She wondered if Ray would still be at the prison. He'd been due to finish on Wednesday and be on a week's leave, but knowing him there's a chance he would've stayed on. Especially if they've had staff issues too.

She looked at the fuel range indicator and did some mental maths. It was a bit of a detour, but she decided she'd enough petrol to cover it. She wanted to know if her brother was there or not. She certainly didn't want to land at her parent's and find that he wasn't home.

Lisa slowed to a crawl as she approached the front gate of the prison. The huge metal gates rose menacingly, reminding her of the iconic entrance from the Jurassic Park movie. Both were designed to keep the inhabitants locked securely inside. *Until the electricity goes off*, she thought. The dark-clouded sky cast the structure as cold and heavy and lifeless.

She'd only been here two or three times, to either pick Ray up or to drop something off to him. Each time, if she remembered correctly, the large outer gate had been open, with a traffic barrier down on the other side, manned by a security guard.

That wasn't the case today. There was no guard in sight, and both the outer gate and its twin, about a twenty yards further in, were closed.

She pulled her car into a lay-by across from the small guardhouse to the side of the main gate.

As she approached, the gates and the razor wire-topped fence loomed above her. It was an ominous sight. With every step, she became smaller, and the feeling of apprehension grew. She couldn't imagine how the approach would feel for someone who was about to be a long-term guest.

When she got to within ten yards of the guardhouse, she noticed something out of the ordinary. There was a sheet of A4 paper taped to the small window, one corner flapping in the breeze. It had a message handwritten in thick black marker. She slowed and squinted to try to read the message.

As her focus dialled in, something else appeared in the window. A face.

The thick steel door beside the window swung open, and a man stepped out. Lisa immediately recoiled. He wasn't in the expected prison guard uniform. Even someone in a suit would've been acceptable. He was dressed in well-worn, grey, cotton tracksuit pants and a tight blue sweatshirt, and had a polished bald head.

"Alright love," said the man, in a thick Belfast accent, as he emerged from the door. Lisa took an involuntary step backwards.

Two other men followed the first out of the guardhouse. The first was a short, round bull of a man, all shoulders and no neck. The next guy was taller, dressed a little neater in a light blue shirt. He had short, grey hair, which probably added to his air of authority.

The tall grey-haired man smiled, which accentuated a nasty looking facial scar. "It's alright love, sorry if we alarmed you," he said, as the three men slowly edged forward.

Lisa continued to take small steps back. She fought the urge to look round at her car.

The tall man continued in a civil tone, "We're contractors working in the prison during the power cut," he said, still smiling. The other two nodded and smiled, too.

Bullshit, thought Lisa. She could feel her heart thundering in her chest.

"Would you be able to give us a lift into Belfast, by any chance?" he said. "Our van broke down." He could see that his ruse wasn't working, and the three of them hastened their advance slightly.

At that instant, the facade of civility shattered, and Lisa turned and sprinted for her car.

She hit the key fob as she ran, and the lights flashed.

She could feel the presence of at least one pursuer close behind her. She dared not to look back. Focus, focus.

At any second, she expected to feel a hand yank her by the hair, or to be tackled to the ground. She willed her legs to keep pumping.

The car was passenger side-on to her.

Do I go round the front or the back? Front or back?

She focused on what she needed to do.

Round the bonnet, open the door, jump in, lock the door.

She was sure the hand was nearly on her. She wanted to look back.

She could hear him breathing.

She wanted to duck.

Front.

She reached the car and slide her hands across the bonnet to slow her momentum. She allowed herself a glance as she turned.

He was there, right there. Three feet. Two feet. Within arm's length. He had her.

As she reached for the handle of the door, she expected her arm to be ripped away.

He too used the bonnet to slow himself for the turn, but as he rounded on her, his foot caught the curb and he tumbled. He rolled on to the grass verge.

Where's the other one?

Lisa grabbed at the handle and looked over the roof. The bull was charging. His arms were out to the sides, giving his girth space to churn as his legs did their best to keep him in the chase.

He was close, but she could make it.

The fast bald one regained his footing.

Get the door closed, get the door closed. Lisa was certain that a hand would grab the door before she got it slammed shut. He was right there.

He must've missed the handle by a fraction of an inch as Lisa jerked it shut and clicked the lock button on the key fob. Looking in a panic to make sure she'd hit the right button.

The instant she heard the click of the lock, she saw him tugging on the handle. On the passenger side, the fat bull slammed into the passenger door. His sweaty pink hands slapped on the window.

"Open the fucking door, you bitch," he screamed, his face about to explode.

Lisa scrambled with the fob and unfolded the key. She allowed herself a quick look to her right. Where did he go?

She jammed the key in the ignition and turned.

The window beside her exploded, and her head snapped to the side. She stomped on the accelerator as the bald guy's hand grabbed for the steering wheel. The car lurched forward, and he lost his grip. He hopped and then sprinted alongside the car, his face twisted in rage.

Lisa accelerated hard, the engine screaming for her to change gear. A glance in her mirror confirmed that the bald one and the fat one had given up their chase after a few yards. The tall guy stood with hands on hips. He hadn't taken up the futile chase. All three faded into the distance as she raced away.

The wind rushed through the missing window and a blanket of tiny glass cubes covered the interior of the car and pooled in her lap.

She moved her right hand from her head to the steering wheel and changed into third; the engine took a relieved breath.

The wheel was now slick under her hand but turning sticky. The blood was running freely. She could feel it on her cheek and on her neck and inside the collar of her blouse. Her right eye was blurred. She wiped it with the relatively blood-free back of her hand to try to keep her vision clear.

She drove on, telling herself to breathe and drive more slowly.

A tight bend nearly took her by surprise on the desolate country road, forcing her to ease back on the pedal. Her heart raced, and her head throbbed with every beat. She was tired. So tired. Her mouth was dry. The frigid air rushing in did little to keep her eyes from growing heavy.

As the road straightened in front of her, a small house appeared in the distance.

The right side of her face was painted in drying blood. *I'm Two-Face, from Batman*, she thought, horrified by her reflection in the mirror.

Thankfully, she hadn't got any blood on her favourite dressing gown; it felt nice and cosy, the soft cotton warming her against the rushing air.

She blinked, barely able to see now from her right eye, the treacle-like blood slowly gluing it shut. Everything was heavy. She caught herself fighting to keep her chin from dropping. A shake of her head was rewarded with a stab of pain and reverberating throb in her temple.

Her hands clung tightly to the steering wheel, still no blood on the fluffy cuffs of her dressing gown nor on her thick warm duvet, which she was so happy to snuggle down into. She loved her bed.

The brilliant white pillow appeared in an instant in front of her face and embraced her with a slap and then flattened.

###

She could hear the sound of her parent's old whistling kettle nearing the boil, when a large rough hand took her by the arm and shook her rudely.

"Daddy?" she croaked.

"It's okay love, you're okay, don't worry, I've got you," said the elderly man attached to the hand. "I'm gonna get you out. Can you tell me if you're in pain anywhere?"

"Five more minutes, Daddy," she pleaded, and fell back to sleep.

CHAPTER 30

Anger had finally dragged Simon from his coma of grief.

He'd allowed Derek and Jenny to help him clean his friend's blood from him as best they could, and had dressed in fresh clothes.

They'd reluctantly gone to bed, giving in to exhaustion, but he couldn't. He paced the apartment, cycling through phases of crippling despair and sadness, blood boiling rage, and soul-crushing guilt. He knew who'd done this. *It was those fucking junkies*, he thought. *It had to be them*.

He stood on the balcony looking down to where, just hours before, his closest friend had died in his arms. He gripped the metal railing so tight that his hands ached and stared across at the entrance to Heroin Heights.

Seamus' wooden cudgel dangled from his wrist, still stained with the blood of its owner. If Simon had his way, it would be soaked in the blood of Martin's murderers by the end of the night. If the police weren't gonna do anything about it, he'd do it himself.

He wanted to go over and kick in every door until he found them. Derek had physically stopped him at one point and talked reason to him. It was now looking like a viable solution again. But no one had come or gone to the apartment block across the street in the hours that he'd kept vigil. The place was quiet and dark, as was the street.

He looked down at the gate again where Martin had been killed. If only he'd heard him calling his name sooner. If only he'd got down the stairs faster. Fat, useless prick.

A wave of grief and exhaustion gripped him, and he abandoned his post. He slumped into the chair by the window in the living room and looked out at the shimmering river.

The dawn light eased him awake. For the briefest of moments, in the space between being asleep and awake, he thought everything had been a horrible, twisted nightmare. He thought that the lights would work, that he'd be served by Seamus in the shop, and that his friend Martin would call, as he did most days. The pain of realisation, when it came, pinned him to the chair. Floods of uncontrollable tears streamed down his face, and he held his head in his hands. His friend was gone.

A flash of anger and determination spurred him to move, and he returned to the balcony to keep watch for the murdering drug addicts.

As dawn broke and the streets below brightened, he saw a car pull up at the curb outside Heroin Heights. It wasn't Martin's car, and he didn't recognise the male and female who got out of the back seat. He watched intently as they moved to the boot and recovered two large cardboard boxes full of… stuff. He couldn't see what it was, but it could've been Martin's supplies.

Before the car drove off, another figure emerged from the passenger seat. It was Fat Head, the junkie prick that he'd seen many times; dancing or fighting or begging. *I bet it was him*; he thought.

He turned to go, just as Derek appeared at the balcony door.

"Hey Simon," said Derek quietly. "Did you get any sleep?"

"It's them, it's fucking them, they've got his stuff!" screamed Simon hysterically.

"What? Stop, Simon," said Derek, stepping out onto the balcony.

"It was that bubble-headed bastard. I know it was him," he said, his voice breaking with rage and desperation.

Derek looked down as the front door of the apartment block closed behind the returning residents.

"It's fucking them," said Simon, waving his arms. "We have to do something."

"What do you suppose we do, Simon?" said Derek sternly.

"We fuckin' kill the fuckers."

Derek stared at him and said nothing.

"You've got guns," said Simon, looking back into the apartment. "Give me one." He moved to force his way past Derek, who grabbed him by the arms.

"Okay, that's enough," shouted Derek. "What happened to your friend was awful, and the fact that the police can't do anything about it right now is terrible, but you can't go over there and start fucking killing people. Are you mad?"

Simon was trembling with rage.

"There's no way to know who did it. Nobody saw them," said Derek.

Simon glared at him, then looked at the ground. He knew Derek was right. He knew he was being irrational.

"Come on, I'll make some coffee."

"There's no milk," said Simon, defeated.

"We'll have black coffee then," said Derek.

"I don't think there's even any water left."

"We'll use river water then."

Simon looked at him and winced. "Are you serious?"

"No," said Derek with a slight smile.

"I've nothing left in the cupboards," said Simon. He felt and sounded pathetic. "I don't know what I'm gonna do."

Jenny appeared behind them at the kitchen door. "You'll come with us to Donegal," she said, and looked to Derek for affirmation.

"Yeah, you can come with us," said Derek. "And when everything's working again, we'll

come back and go to the police about Martin
and Seamus."

Simon looked at Derek and then at Jenny and
nodded slowly.

CHAPTER 31

Lisa heard the world around her before she saw it. As she focused on the harsh light from the window, she was greeted by the smiling eyes of a grey-breaded face. The man's eyes shone with kindness, but the map of deep creases around them told of worry and pain. His light wisps of white hair had their own ideas on neatness, personal grooming clearly lower on the man's list of daily chores.

He looked down at her like a dentist. "There you are," he said in a coarse but soothing voice.

As he reached to adjust the cold, wet cloth that lay across her forehead, she recoiled slightly and was rewarded with a bolt of pain from her temple that travelled through her entire body.

"It's okay, you've had a bit of a bang on the head," he said.

She looked at him, confused.

"You crashed your car, do you remember?" he said.

She remembered the prison; the men chasing her, speeding away in her car. She moved to rise from the couch that she'd been reclined on.

"Take it easy," he said, taking her gently by the arm and helping her to sit up. "You've a nasty cut on your head. I think you'll need some stitches."

"Where am I?"

"You crashed into my gate post. I brought you in and patched you up, but it's only temporary. I'm George. What's your name, love?"

"How far am I from the prison?"

George frowned, "Maghaberry?"

"Yes, how far is it?"

"About four miles. Why?"

"They attacked me. I think they're escaped prisoners."

George's frown deepened, his forehead resembling that of a curious pug.

"There were three of them. They smashed my window with a rock or something," said Lisa, tentatively raising her fingers to the now bandaged cut on her temple.

"We have to phone the police," she said, as she tried to stand, immediately regretting it, as a wave of dizziness and nausea hit her.

"Okay, you stay there, I'll try to call them, but I wouldn't hold out much hope, I've been trying to get through to the doctor's and the chemist, and even the hospital, and can't get anyone," said George.

He moved through to the kitchen and lifted the receiver from the wall-mounted telephone. It had one of those long receiver leads that stretched all the way back into the living room.

"You phoned the hospital for me?" asked Lisa when he returned.

"No love, for my wife," he said, lowering his voice, "she's in bed. She's very poorly, and we've nearly run out of her pain medication."

"Oh," said Lisa, an attempt at a sympathetic frown causing another stab of pain.

"She suffered a stroke last year," he said. "She's not doing too good."

George dialled 999 and shook his head. "I'm on hold," he said, pulling his pug face again. "It's been like this for me the last couple of days."

"Come on through and I'll make you a cup of tea," said George.

Lisa followed him through to the kitchen and sat at the small table.

"Is your door locked?" she asked. "They might be coming this way. They wanted my car, I think."

"Yes, love, the door's locked. Don't worry."

She was worried, and it was showing on her face. She jumped when she heard a thump from behind her. "What was that?" She stood and turned to face the door leading to the hall.

"It's okay, that just my Rose," he said with a smile. "I'll just go and check on her. Can you listen on here in case they answer?"

He handed her the ancient telephone receiver and adjusted the kettle on the gas stove before heading out into the hall. It reminded her of her mum's kettle, with the little whistle cap on the spout.

She listened to the crackly recording of classical music on the phone. *I didn't know you could be put on hold on a 999 call*; she thought.

The stairs creaked with every laboured step that George took as he slowly ascended to tend to his wife.

Lisa moved back into the living room. She wanted to look out the front window. The telephone cord was long, but it didn't quite stretch to the window. She took it to its outer range, pulling the coiled wire straight, then held it at arm's length to give herself another couple of feet.

She tried to focus through the patterned lace curtains. She saw her car, or at least a yellow blur that was her car, but she couldn't see much else.

She listened on the phone again, still on hold. She examined the phone for a speaker function, with no success. Some of the buttons had their markings worn off. It might've been one of those.

Tucking the phone behind a cushion on the armchair, she decided to take the chance. She pulled the curtain back, releasing a cloud of vintage dust, and looked out.

Her poor wee car was a right off, the concrete gate was embedded deep into the engine block, the bonnet folded like a yellow napkin around it.

She panned her view back along the road in the direction she'd come. Her heart jumped to her throat. Three figures had just crested the small hill about two hundred yards from the house. She instinctively took a step back.

"Everything okay?" said George from behind her. "Any answer yet?" he said, looking at the phone stuffed down behind the pillow.

The words made her jump. "They're coming," she said. "That's them."

George approached the window and narrowed his eyes. He tutted and looked around the room. "I need my other glasses."

"It's them, I'm telling you." Lisa was nearing hysterics. "They're gonna see my car and come in here."

The spike in adrenaline had her pacing back and forth. Her attention darted around the room, fight-or-flight instinct telling her to hide behind the sofa or grab the poker from the fireplace.

"It's okay, love. What's your name anyway, love?" said George, his seeming lack of concern heightening her panic.

"Lisa," she said, "my name's Lisa. We need to hide."

"Okay Lisa, it's gonna be alright. I'll not let them hurt you," he said calmly.

George led her through into the kitchen. He ducked through a narrow door into what looked like a larder, and after a few seconds came out with a massive double-barrelled shotgun. Her father had a shotgun, but it was nowhere near the size of this thing.

George set the gun on the kitchen table and proceeded to extract two buckshot cartridges from a cardboard box. The process was painfully slow. He plucked awkwardly at the shells, his mottled and fragile hands no longer as responsive as they'd once been.

He set the two cartridges carefully on their ends on the table.

For fuck's sake, hurry up! Lisa screamed in her head.

Lifting the heavy shotgun like he had all the time in the world, he pushed the top lever to open the barrel. He balanced it across his right arm and lifted the first cartridge. The old man moved in slow motion. She wanted to grab the shells and pop them in the gun herself. Pop, pop, done.

As George finally slid the first shell home, they heard a knock on the front door. Not a heavy or demanding bang, just a standard knock, knock, knock. George and Lisa looked at each other, expressionless.

He resumed loading the gun, a little faster this time, to his credit. Another, more forceful, summons to the door echoed through the house, as George snapped the gun closed.

"It's okay," said George, still calm and reassuring. "If we just stay in here, they'll move on." He moved to the kitchen door and edged it open an inch to look down the hall.

A pair of eyes glaring through the skinny pane of the back door made Lisa scream, "George, there!"

George turned.

The back door splintered as the bull-like convict shouldered his way through it. Glass and wood sprayed in all directions. The intruder bellowed as he took one crunching step into George's kitchen. His war-cry was immediately cut short, silenced by the deafening blast of the shotgun.

A dinner plate sized crater appeared in the centre of the man's chest. His forward charge halted in an instant by the power of the point-blank explosion. With one staggering step backwards, he tumbled out through the door.

Lisa couldn't hear her own screams. The thunderous blast and blinding flash, followed by the acrid smell of burning gunpowder, overloaded her senses. She was frozen to the spot, fists clenched and shaking.

In the din of deafening silence, she saw the hallway door fling open. George sensed it too and spun as fast as his ageing reflexes would allow. His finger squeezed on the second trigger as the new intruder drove the barrel sky-wards.

In an instant, the two men were toe to toe, engulfed in a cloud of plaster dust and ceiling confetti.

The grey-haired prisoner wrestled the gun from his elderly opponent with ease. He shoved George backwards before jabbing the butt of the huge gun into his stomach.

George let out a groan and crumpled to one knee.

With a savage downward chop, the younger man brought the stock down on George's head. The old man fell silent and slumped to the ground beside Lisa.

With a sudden violent urge, Lisa lunged at the tall attacker. She swung a balled fist at his face, the blow glancing off his cheek as he deftly shifted his weight.

She stumbled past him and turned to pounce again. As she wound up her second attack, an unseen hand grabbed her by the hair and rammed her face first into the wall before reversing the direction and whipping her across the room.

She slid across the kitchen table and crashed through a chair before coming to rest on the floor beside the unconscious pensioner.

Lisa lay still, her face pressed against the cold tile floor.

Without lifting her head, she watched the grey tracksuit legs rush to the back door.

"He's fuckin' dead," he shouted from just outside the door. "They fuckin' killed Sammy."

"Fuck," said the blue jeans.

The tracksuit returned, "Fuckin' do him. Do them both. They fuckin' killed him."

"Shut up," said blue jeans, obviously in charge. "Look for car keys for the Škoda."

"What about Sammy?"

"Get the fucking car keys first."

Lisa pushed herself slowly to a seated position against the washing machine.

The bald man stepped closer to her. "Where's the fuckin' car keys, bitch?"

She shook her head.

"Where's the keys?" his face was red with murderous rage.

"I don't know. I don't live here," said Lisa, edging away.

"Go and look in the other room," said the grey-haired boss.

The bald one left the room. His boss crouched down beside George and shook him roughly. There was no reaction from George.

He turned his back and started rummaging through drawers, tossing their contents on the floor.

Lisa slowly manoeuvred her feet under her and, like a sprinter from the blocks, bolted for the door to the hall.

As she passed the living room door, the bald man crashed into her, sending her skidding along the wood-floored hall.

She clawed and scrambled along the hall, trying to regain her feet. She felt a hand grab her ankle and yank her backwards. Spinning on to her back, she kicked out at her attacker. The kicks were met with a sneer as he dragged her closer.

CHAPTER 32

Derek couldn't allow himself to go to Donegal without checking the prison again. He had to know whether the army had turned up and taken control. If they had, he'd leave the weapons with them. Although given the events of the previous day, he was feeling more inclined to hold on to them.

If he was caught over the border with firearms, there'd be no doubt he'd lose his job, at the very least, but that was now likely to happen anyway, so what'd he have to lose?

There weren't many cars on the roads, but there was a steady stream of people on foot. All but a few, heading in the opposite direction to them, towards City Hall and the food supplies that they so desperately needed.

"Everyone okay?" asked Derek, looking through the rear-view mirror at his wife and then at Simon in the passenger seat.

"Yip," said Jenny with a smile.

"You okay, Simon?"

Simon stared out the window, then eventually turned and nodded. "Yeah."

Derek couldn't imagine the sense of helplessness that Simon must've been feeling. The anger and frustration. He knew he'd feel the same if his friend had died in his arms. It was the right thing to do, to take him with them. He was sure Ray's parents wouldn't mind one more guest; they were always so welcoming.

As he pulled off the motorway and on to the familiar approach road to the prison, he felt his stomach tighten. The clouds were closing in and darkening. Dread had glued his jaw tight.

He begged the universe that when he saw the gates to his prison, he'd also see army vehicles and guards in green camouflage. The alternative was unfathomable, that the men he was entrusted to guard, and to keep safe, were still locked inside and quickly running out of food. How could he go to Donegal and just pretend that nine hundred men weren't starving to death in a cage? A cage that he had locked.

As he rounded the corner and the huge gates came into sight, he could see that the outer gate was still shut. *But that doesn't mean the army isn't there*, he told himself.

The closer he got, the quicker the hope ebbed from him. There were no soldiers on guard at the gate. *They might all be inside*, he thought.

"What do you think?" said Jenny.

"Not sure yet," said Derek. "Doesn't look good, though." There, he'd admitted it. No point kidding himself anymore. The army wasn't there. He could see the thick chain and padlock still securing the main gate.

He pulled up a few yards from the gatehouse. The message he'd taped to the window was still there.

He got out of the car, not knowing what further confirmation he needed, but he approached the guardhouse anyway.

He stopped short. The guardhouse door was open. It shouldn't be open. He looked around nervously. Retreating quickly, he got into the car and locked the doors without a word.

"Well?" said Jenny.

"They're not there yet," he said. "Maybe they'll get there later today or tomorrow." *Jesus, what have I done?* he thought.

"So, what now?" said Jenny.

Derek let out a deep sigh. "We go to Donegal."

"What about the guns?" asked Jenny.

Derek looked at her in the mirror and shrugged. "We take them with us."

He looked at the guardhouse door again and then with a slow blink; he turned a page and drove off.

They drove in silence for a few minutes. Derek was on autopilot, the jury in his head deciding his fate and the judge passing an appropriately stiff sentence.

Simon leaned forward in his seat and squinted through the windscreen. "That looks like your friend Lisa's car."

Derek was only half listening and by the time he'd dialled in, he was past the car.

"I think it is," said Simon. "I saw her in it the other night."

Derek applied the brakes, and they came to a stop about twenty yards past the scene of the crash. He wasn't sure if he knew what Lisa drove. He thought he'd remember if it was a slap in the face, bright-yellow Beetle.

Jenny twisted around in her seat and looked back at the car. "Oh my God, it is Lisa's car."

Derek reversed and stopped a few feet from the front of the crashed car.

Derek and Simon got out and approached the car, while Jenny stood by her door.

"Shit, she hit that at some speed," said Simon, looking at the damage to the small car.

Derek examined the driver side window. "This is strange."

"What is it?"

"The side window's smashed," said Derek, as he leaned in through the broken window. "There's a fair amount of blood."

"Did you say there was blood?" said Jenny, straining to hear.

"Yes," said Derek. He straightened and looked up at the house. "I wonder if she's in there? They'll hopefully know something at least," he said.

"Can you pull the car up to that lay by please Simon?" he said, pointing back to his own car, which was blocking most of the road.

The two men jumped when a boom echoed across the valley. Birds in the nearby trees took flight and scattered into the sky.

"What the fuck was that?" said Simon.

Derek starred up at the house and looked at Simon, his brow narrowed. "It came from the house."

At that moment, a second shot rang out. "Stay with the car, move it up the road a bit," said Derek.

"Where're you going?" shouted Jenny.

"Just stay in the car."

Derek jogged up the short driveway. He held his breath and could feel his heart racing. The front door was ajar, and the wood around the lock was cracked and splintered.

He saw the shadows of movement in the dim hall as he got closer. A fight.

Derek angled his head and cautiously peered through the small opening. He eased the door open with his hand. Halfway along the hall, he saw a red-haired woman squirming and thrashing, pinned down by the weight of a large bald man. He knew the man; he knew the woman, Lisa.

"Lisa," Derek shouted. "Get the fuck off her!"

The bald man was pressing down with both hands on Lisa's throat. At the sound of the shout, he looked up. The appearance of the black figure, silhouetted in the doorway, caused him to pause just long enough for Lisa to rotate her body and break his grip.

Derek reached under his left arm and drew his gun.

With her freed hand Lisa drove straight up and connected with a hollow thud just above the man's Adam's Apple. He let out an involuntary croak and reared back.

Derek's gun was either unseen or ignored by the enraged prisoner. He snatched a cast iron doorstop, which lay by the cloakroom door beside him, and raised it up, ready to strike.

Two sharp cracks reverberated down the hall. The bald prisoner jerked twice, the doorstop tumbling to the ground as a pair of coin-sized holes blossomed in the centre of his chest.

Lisa kicked and twisted her way free as her attacker slumped to the ground beside her, clutching his chest and wheezing his last breath. She turned and looked up, glassy-eyed.

Derek crouched down beside her. "Lisa, it's okay, it's okay."

She stared at him, her face twisted in pain and astonishment. "Derek?" the sound barely making it out of her bruised and swollen throat.

"It's okay."

She gestured wildly and pointed towards the kitchen. "Another one..."

As Derek looked up a heavy blow struck him across the face. He drove himself upwards and speared the man back through the kitchen door.

A tight grip prevented him from raising his gun as the two men grappled and stumbled across the kitchen.

Derek's head ground into his opponent's temple as he strained every muscle to gain purchase. The stench of sweat and blood and hot, putrid breath filled his nostrils. In a grunting, cursing tangle, the two powerful men thrashed in tight circles around the kitchen.

Their heads came apart just long enough for Derek to identify the assailant. The sight of Baker flared his rage and determination.

In a desperate move, Derek pivoted, trying to use Baker's weight against him. It worked. The tall grey-haired prisoner spun and lost his balance. Derek turned his body and thrust his hip into the man to aid his descent.

Baker went down hard, but his grip on Derek's right arm was vice-like, and it dragged him forward.

Derek crashed through a wooden kitchen chair and landed with a slap on the tiled floor, his right arm trapped under him. The gun was gone. He heard it skid across the floor, out of sight.

Rolling onto his back, Derek tried to sit up, his mind searching for Baker. A hard, muscular forearm closed around his neck as his head was wrenched backwards by the hair.

He had seconds. *If I let this fucker lock me into a chokehold it'll be all over*, thought Derek, *I'll be dead*. He curled his fingers into the crook of Baker's elbow and yanked down as hard as he could, giving himself a vital inch of breathing space.

He reached behind blindly and found a handful of shirt collar. With all the force he could muster, he hauled the man forward as he drove his knee upwards. The crunch of cartilage was sickening as Baker's nose shattered.

Derek's feet skidded on the smooth tiles as he tried to rise. He was halfway up when Baker's full weight collapsed on him. Derek crumpled.

Baker was on him in an instant, astride him, pinning him to the ground and raining hammer-heavy blows down on his face and head. Derek curled his arms up and deflected some of the deadly strikes with his elbows and arms, but he was weakening.

In slow motion, Derek saw Baker rearing up to deliver what he knew would be the finishing blow.

Thud... thud... the echoing sound of wood rebounding off the back of Baker's head marked Derek's reprieve.

Baker rose and flung his arm in a wide circle to try to fend off another of Simon's savage strikes. He managed to deflect the third swing and lunged forward, driving his forehead into Simon's cheekbone, before falling back against the draining board. Blood fountained down his face.

Simon regained his composure and stepped in again, all his frustration, all his anger, all his grief crammed into Seamus's eighteen-inch hardwood cudgel.

Baker snatched a bread knife from the counter beside him and sliced in a wide arc towards Simon. Simon halted and took a half step back, the club raised above his head.

Baker glared down at Derek, lying battered and defenceless at his feet. He moved to strike.

Crack, crack, crack. Two of the bullets punched through Baker, one in the neck and one up through his ribs.

George lay propped on one elbow, his frail, shaking hand still extended, the Glock 26 at the end.

Trevor Baker fell like a tree, his bloodied face coming to rest inches from Derek's. The two men locked eyes. Derek watched as the inmate's pupils widened and froze.

CHAPTER 33

Lisa rocked gently, her knees drawn up. She shook uncontrollably. The man with the wooden club appeared in the kitchen doorway. He clenched the deadly weapon by his side. *Martin's friend? What the fuck?* She didn't understand what was happening.

"It's okay, Lisa," said Simon. "It's over. You're okay."

"Where's Derek?" asked Lisa, her throat stinging with every word.

"He's okay," said Simon, before turning and returning to the kitchen.

Derek steadied himself on the door frame and shuffled down the hall, staring down as he stepped over the man he'd killed.

Lisa pushed herself to her feet and hugged her big brother's best friend. His face was bruised and cut.

"It's okay," he said. "Come with me. Jenny's out in the car." He led her out into the driveway.

"Why? How are you here?" she said, confusion overwhelming her.

Jenny stood at the end of the driveway, hands pressed to her head. She saw Derek and ran to him. Alarm and relief fought for control of her features when she saw his cut and battered face.

"Oh my God, your face. What the hell happened, Derek?"

"It's okay, love, we're all okay."

Lisa stood wide eyed. "They were from the prison."

"I know," said Derek.

Jenny held her hands gently to her husband's face. "What happened?"

"I'll tell you in a minute," he said. "Take Lisa to the car."

"No, I have to see if George is okay," said Lisa, turning to re-enter the house.

"He's fine," said Derek. "He saved us."

Lisa ignored him and returned to the house, summoning all her strength to step past the dead body in the hall. The kitchen was a war zone. The grey-haired prisoner lay on his side, unmoving, dead.

Simon was helping George to his feet. He supported the old man and helped him through to the living room. Lisa hugged herself tightly and followed them.

"Are you okay, George?" asked Lisa.

"Yes love, I'm fine. Did they hurt you?"

"I'm okay," said Lisa, despite every word coming with a swallow of broken glass.

She turned to Simon, who looked surprisingly calm.

"How are *you* here?" she said.

"I'm going to Donegal with Derek and Jenny."

"To my house?" asked Lisa. This doesn't make any sense. What the fuck is going on? she thought.

"Where's Martin?" she asked. "How do you know Derek?"

"It's a long story. I'll tell you later," said Simon solemnly.

"Can you help me upstairs please son?" said George, trying to rise again from the chair, "I need to check on my Rose."

They'd spent the next hour waiting again on hold for the emergency services. Still no answer. Derek moved between the house and his family in the car.

"We need to leave," said Derek. "If these guys got out of the prison, others will have too."

Simon nodded.

"Do you have somewhere you can go, George?" asked Lisa.

George shook his head. "I'm not going anywhere. This's my home."

"You can't stay here," said Derek.

"Listen son, my wife is in her last days. She can't be moved."

"There could be more prisoners coming this way," said Derek in protest.

"Let them come. I've killed two of them. I'll kill the rest. This is my home."

Derek closed his eyes and shook his head.

"You can't stay here on your own," said Lisa.

"I've got my Rose, and I've got my shotgun," he said with a smile.

"But do me a favour, though, before you go?" George said, turning to Simon and Derek. "Get these fuckers out of my house!"

Simon looked at the grey track suit legs that were visible through the living room door.

"Pile them out the front. That should stop any other boyos from trying anything."

George looked again at Lisa, "Don't worry love, I'll get through to the police at some stage. It'll be okay. You need to go before it gets dark."

CHAPTER 34

Every footstep caused the wound on Lisa's head to pound as they tracked along the winding country road. The pace had slowed to a crawl.

They walked in near silence, each deep in their own thoughts, trying to process the traumatic events of the day.

Lisa's feet were heavy as she followed closely behind Jenny. She was envious of the sleeping baby in the pram, who was oblivious to the pain and anguish that the adults around him had suffered.

Behind her, Derek struggled too under the heavy load of the backpack, hunched high on his shoulders, and the duffel bag of prison weapons cradled in his arms. She could hear his panting and an occasional grunt when he readjusted his load.

"Are you sure I can't take something and give you a bit of a break?" Lisa asked as she turned and waited for Derek to catch up. She had her own bag, but she thought she could manage another, even for a short distance.

"No, it's fine thanks, sure it's not that far now. Sure it isn't?" he said. It was hard to tell exactly in the dark, and Derek wasn't overly familiar with the roads.

"No, about a mile," said Lisa.

Up ahead, Simon fared no better under his own heavy rucksack. The dark clouds had drawn across the sky and blocked out the moonlight. The only thing lighting their path now was the small torch on Simon's wind up radio, which cast a dim but welcome arc in front of them.

The car had finally given up just past the last small village. It'd choked on the last of the fumes from the petrol tank and died. They'd all been focused on the fuel indicator on the dashboard for the last half of the journey. She now understood the range-anxiety that all electric car owners supposedly had, as she watched the mileage counter tick down to zero.

The car journey from George's house had been quiet and thankfully uneventful. They'd taken the back roads, mostly, to avoid the towns. The only nervous moment had been when they approached a small town where a group of men had set up a roadblock.

Derek had told them to get ready to duck. He wasn't gonna stop for anything and had been ready to burst through the unofficial checkpoint. As they got closer, they saw that the men were armed, but thankfully they waved the car on without stopping it, seemingly happy that the occupants weren't looters or joyriders.

She sometimes saw the trip home as a bit of a chore, and more than once she'd given her parents some excuse for why she wouldn't be visiting at the weekend, preferring to enjoy a fun-filled weekend without somewhere to be. She could think of no better sight now than that of the tall stone pillars at the gate of her parents' farm and the familiar bone rattling she'd get as she crossed the cattle grill.

She wanted to hug her parents and her brother Ray and feel the safety of her childhood home. She knew she was among friends now, both old and new, but she needed to be with her family and away from the world that had turned mad overnight.

When they reached the top of the hill, Lisa quickened her pace and caught up with Simon.

"Hey, how're you holding up?" she asked.

"Okay, is it much further?" he said, breathing heavily. The lump over his eye had swollen badly, like in a cartoon, and he had to turn his head fully to see her.

"Not far now, about twenty minutes, I think. That looks sore."

"It's okay."

"Thank you again for what you did back there," she said with a smile. "You saved our lives."

"I think Derek did most of the saving," he said, returning her smile.

"I'm glad you were there," she said. "I'm sorry about Martin. He was a really good man."

Simon looked at the ground and nodded.

"What kind of farm do your parents have?" asked Simon. He clearly wanted to change the subject.

"It used to be a small dairy farm, but they only have a handful of cows now," said Lisa. "My dad's mostly retired. They still supply some vegetables and eggs to the local shops."

She lost her footing and stumbled. Simon caught her arm and helped steady her. "Are you okay? You look in bad shape yourself, you might be concussed."

"I'm a wee bit dizzy, but I'll be okay."

Simon was still holding her by the arm when they saw headlights in the distance. She felt his grip tighten, and he edged her in closer.

Derek approached from the rear and ushered them to the side of the road. "Stay in close to the side. Simon, raise the light up and make sure they see us."

Night turned to day as the car drew nearer. The blinding lights coming dangerously close before the vehicle finally veered out and slowed to a near stop. Three men stared out, displaying no hint of civility. Each occupant of the battered 4x4 glared at the dazzled bystanders — studying, assessing — before accelerating away into the returning darkness.

The group of reluctant hikers paused for a moment by the side of the road and watched the red taillights disappear around a corner before resuming their tiring trek.

Simon was happy that Lisa had stayed beside him for the rest of the walk. He guessed she didn't need his arm to steady her, but he didn't complain. Feeling her beside him was comforting. Without these new friends, he was sure that he'd still be slumped at his kitchen table in the darkness.

"We're nearly there," said Lisa. "It's those white pillars."

"Thank God," said Simon, "I'm not sure I could go on much further."

As they approached the laneway to the farmhouse, he noticed that the gates were closed and locked with a chain. On the other side was a black car parked sideways across the gates, preventing them from being opened.

Simon looked at Derek and frowned.

A chest-high wall extended a few yards to either side of the gateposts before tapering down to meet a wire fence that ran along the hedgerow. There was no way they were gonna be able to get the pram and the baby over the wall.

"I'll go up and get them to move the car," said Lisa.

She set her bag down and moved to the lowest part of the wall. "Could you give me a leg up, Simon?"

"Sure, I'll come with you."

"As quick as you can please, Lisa," said Derek, looking back down the road.

The light from the small torch on the front of his windup radio was starting to fade. He'd charged it using the USB charger in the car, but the battery must've been nearly done. He unfolded the small arm and began cranking it as he and Lisa made their way up the winding, loose-stone driveway.

He saw the large rectangular farmhouse silhouetted by the faint moonlight that'd begun to seep through the thinning clouds. It was a large building with a small set of steps leading up to the front door. To the side loomed the black shadow of a large metal shed. The house looked cold and dark.

Lisa ran ahead and knocked on the over-sized front door. She hardly waited a second before turning and heading for the left side of the building. "I'll try the back door," she said and disappeared around the corner.

Simon waited by the foot of the steps and turned to look back along the short driveway. The lock on the door clicked behind him.

As he turned, he was blinded momentarily by the sharp beam of a flashlight.

"Don't fuckin' move," bellowed a deep voice. "I'll blow your fuckin' head off."

He raised his own small torch, the meagre light from which was swallowed by the much stronger beam.

Another light appeared at the right-hand corner of the house and a younger voice joined the shouts.

"We warned you fuckers to stay off our property," shouted the younger man.

With the added light, Simon could now see that two long barrel guns were levelled at his head.

"I'm with Lisa," he said shakily, raising his hands high in the air.

"Daddy, it's okay, he's with me," shouted Lisa, coming out through the front door behind her father.

"Lisa?" the flashlight spun away as Lisa's dad turned to see his daughter.

"He's with me," she said again.

"Lisa, honey," said her father. He set the shotgun to the side and grabbed his daughter in a tight hug. Her mother appeared beside her in the doorway and joined in the embrace.

The other flashlight bobbed as the second man approached the door, and Lisa hugged her brother tightly.

"Jesus, are we glad to see you," said her brother.

Simon stood awkwardly, watching the family reunion.

"This's Simon," said Lisa, turning to Simon, who was still standing with his arms in the air even though no guns were pointing at him.

"Hello Simon," said Lisa's father. "You can put your hands down, son."

Simon lowered his hands and smiled.

"I need you to move the car from the gate," said Lisa. "Derek and Jenny are here too."

"Derek?" said Lisa's brother, who quickly ducked inside to get the keys for his car before running off down the lane.

Derek was embraced by the smell of freshly baked bread as he stepped into the kitchen of his friend's family home. The whistle of the kettle on the huge Aga cooker was music to his ears. Ray's mother squeezed him tight before ignoring him to fuss over their baby son.

Vincent Keenan engulfed Derek's hand in his and pulled him in for a tight hug. He thanked him for bringing his daughter home safely, although he was still to hear the full story of just how fortuitous the crossing of their paths had been.

There would be many questions, and likely a lot of tears when the answers were given and the nightmares relived, although he didn't think any of his party would have the energy for that tonight.

He accepted a warm cup of fresh coffee from Ray and took a seat at the table with his weary travel companions.

Lisa and Simon sat across from him, bruised and battered — both physically and emotionally — but safe from any further trauma.

Derek looked at his wife, who was showing off their son to Ray's mum. He choked back tears of relief and smiled as he took a sip of his much-missed coffee.

He knew his worries were far from over, the consequences of his actions still hung heavily around his shoulders, but for now, they were a million miles away. When the lights came back on, if they came back on, he would face his fate.

All that mattered now was that his family was safe, and he knew he could rely on the people around him to keep it that way.

The End

Reviews

I hope you enjoyed Reliance, if you did, please consider leaving a short review. Links to the various sites can be found here
https://linktr.ee/pmcmurrough

No matter how short, reviews are very important for independent authors.
Thank you, I look forward to reading your review.

www.ingramcontent.com/pod-product-compliance
Lightning Source LLC
Chambersburg PA
CBHW061206190726
48288CB00001B/77